Two tales of political intrigue in which the Saint untangles international issues. In THE IMPRUDENT PROFESSOR the free world ignores a professor's brilliant strategy for harnessing solar energy—because of its threat to major oil suppliers. The professor, who lives only for the day his discovery will be put into practice, is deceived into believing in a vision of near-Utopian existence in the Soviet Union. The results might have been disastrous had his beautiful daughter not secured the aid of the illustrious Simon Templar—the Saint.

In THE RED SABBATH, the Saint and Leila, his beautiful Israeli accomplice must track down the head of the Red Sabbath – a group of cold-blooded assassins whose targets are often the defenseless. Even the Saint is not above using the oldest trick in the book and when he discovers that Hakim had a girl in London, he baits his hook. Things proceed rather smoothly, though the beautiful Leila proves to be more difficult than the cold-hearted killer . . .

By Leslie Charteris

DAREDEVIL
THE BANDIT
THE WHITE RIDER
X ESQUIRE

The Saint Series in order of Sequence

MEET THE TIGER!
ENTER THE SAINT
THE SAINT CLOSES THE CASE
THE AVENGING SAINT
FEATURING THE SAINT
ALIAS THE SAINT
THE SAINT MEETS HIS MATCH
THE SAINT V. SCOTLAND YARD
THE SAINT'S GETAWAY
THE SAINT AND MR. TEAL
THE BRIGHTER BUCCANEER
THE SAINT IN LONDON
THE SAINT INTERVENES
THE SAINT GOES ON
THE SAINT IN NEW YORK
THE SAINT OVERBOARD
ACE OF KNAVES
THE SAINT BIDS DIAMONDS
THE SAINT PLAYS WITH FIRE
FOLLOW THE SAINT
THE HAPPY HIGHWAYMAN
THE SAINT IN MIAMI
THE SAINT GOES WEST
THE SAINT STEPS IN
THE SAINT ON GUARD
THE SAINT SEES IT THROUGH
CALL FOR THE SAINT
SAINT ERRANT
THE SAINT IN EUROPE
THE SAINT ON THE SPANISH MAIN
THANKS TO THE SAINT
THE SAINT AROUND THE WORLD
SEÑOR SAINT
THE SAINT TO THE RESCUE
TRUST THE SAINT
THE SAINT IN THE SUN
VENDETTA FOR THE SAINT
THE SAINT ON T.V.
THE SAINT RETURNS
THE SAINT AND THE FICTION MAKERS
THE SAINT ABROAD
THE SAINT'S CHOICE
THE SAINT IN PURSUIT
THE SAINT AND THE PEOPLE IMPORTERS
CATCH THE SAINT
THE SAINT AND THE HAPSBURG NECKLACE
SEND FOR THE SAINT
THE SAINT IN TROUBLE

Leslie Charteris'

The Saint in Trouble

The Imprudent Professor & The Red Sabbath

Two Original Stories by

TERENCE FEELY and JOHN KRUSE

Adapted by

GRAHAM WEAVER

PUBLISHED FOR THE CRIME CLUB BY

DOUBLEDAY & COMPANY, INC.

GARDEN CITY, NEW YORK

1978

All of the characters in this book
are fictitious, and any resemblance
to actual persons, living or dead,
is purely coincidental.

Library of Congress Cataloging in Publication Data

Weaver, Graham.
Leslie Charteris' The Saint in trouble.

(The Saint series)
CONTENTS: The imprudent professor.–The Red Sabbath.
1. Detective and mystery stories, English.
I. Charteris, Leslie, 1907– II. Feely, Terence.
III. Kruse, John. IV. Title. V. Title: The Saint
in trouble.
PZ4.W36284Le 1978 [PR6073.E143] 823'.9'14

ISBN: 0-385-14612-4
Library of Congress Catalog Card Number 78-18551

Printed in the United States of America
First Edition

Contents

Leslie Charteris'

The Saint in Trouble

I

The Imprudent Professor

1

Simon Templar pushed away the remains of his lobster and ordered coffee and cognac. He turned his chair sideways to the table and crossed his legs with careful attention to the crease of his trousers. The brightly colored canvas of the awning overhead offered only token protection from the early afternoon sun, and he envied the customers in the restaurant behind him as they enjoyed the cooler shade of the interior. But his choice of a place outside had been dictated not by considerations of comfort but by its strategic advantage as an observation post.

"An adventurer's life," he telepathically informed the fly sensibly dawdling hopefully in the shadow of his plate, "is not an easy one."

The fly ignored him.

Simon sighed. He was aware that there was a large percentage of the world's population who would gladly have changed places with him. People to whom the prospect of lunching at a luxury restaurant in Cannes on a summer's day would not have seemed an unduly excruciating ordeal. But Simon Templar's moods and opinions rarely coincided with those of the average citizen.

He was also well aware that there were a great many people who would have enjoyed a more contented and peaceful existence had he decided to follow the paths of the majority. Men who would have been happier, richer souls had they never heard of him. Some of whom were known by numbers instead of names and spent their hours sewing containers for Her Majesty's mail.

And there were those too who, had he sought a life checking figures in a ledger, would have been alive to enjoy the sunshine. They knew him not by the names bestowed upon him at his baptism (if there ever had been such a ceremony) but by another that was capable of arousing both hatred and terror; that could start the most secure searching of their passports and the most abject coward looking for a gun. A title that was also synonymous with headaches and discomfiture to the guardians of the law and order in a dozen countries: the Saint.

There had been a time when that name alone was known and the only clue to the identity of its owner was a haloed matchstick figure that might have seemed childish had it not been for the aura of almost supernatural potency that it had acquired. It had been the standard in a private battle against those parasites the police could not touch; a visiting card that carried the same authority as a death warrant.

Official forgiveness from a grateful government for those early sins had not prevented the committing of fresh ones, but the fame that was their inevitable result made the life of a modern buccaneer more complicated than it was comfortable. His reputation brought the Saint adventures he might otherwise have missed, but it also made him the favourite in the chasing-wild-goose stakes and it was in this latter category that he was beginning to place his present business.

In front of him, on the Boulevard de la Croisette, other eaters and drinkers had left their restaurants and cafés and were beginning to pack the pavements again. The road traffic was building up and slowing to a crawl. By turning his head slightly he could forget some of the noise and movement by looking beyond it to the blue waters of the Mediterranean sparkling in the sun.

He watched as a ferry laden with day trippers ploughed from his right towards the islands of Ste. Marguérite and Ste. Honorat on his near horizon, forcing its purposeful passage between the yachts and launches that glided like white-breasted sea birds around the bay. One in particular caught his attention, and he followed its progress for a while as it cruised across his field of view.

It rode high in the water, its knife-sharp bows cutting an easy path for the trim white hull. The flying bridge sprouted enough scanners and antennae to equip a frigate, and the twin screws were using only an infinitesimal fraction of their reserves to push it on its leisured course. By local plutocratic standards it was not a large craft, no more than fifty feet, but its obviously understated power gave it an air of pent-up vitality that had a certain insolent appeal.

The Saint's keen eyes picked out three people on board, the captain on his bridge, a crewman performing some indistinct task in the bow and a girl whose slender form was draped along a lounger on the after deck. As it turned away, perhaps headed for the Port Canto, Simon managed to pick out the name on the transom: *Protégé*. The girl, he was tempted to fantasize, might have been more interesting to protect than the subject he was committed to.

Reluctantly he turned his gaze back along the boulevard to the flag-bedecked Palais des Festivals just across the intervening side street from where he sat. A small group of sombre-suited men stood halfway up the steps. A steady procession of cars and taxis stopped to deposit their similarly unfestive-looking passengers. Each time the same ceremony was repeated: the leader of the greeters, a small bald man with a goatee beard, stepped forward and bowed, shook the hand of the latest arrival, and introduced him to the others. That ceremony over, a uniformed attendant would appear and escort the visitor into the building. A couple of press photographers clicked their cameras without moving from the wall they were supporting. Above the entrance to the Palais was draped a white banner bearing the flaming brand emblem of the European Institute for Scientific Advancement, below which was proclaimed CONGRÈS DE RESSOURCES D'ÉNÉRGIE ALTERNATIVE.

The sight of the precise men performing their precise ritual, coupled with the words on the banner, deepened the frustration that had been building up in him during the three days since his arrival in Cannes.

It was nothing about the town that exasperated him, for it was early enough in the season for there still to be room to stroll the sidewalks, lie on the beach, or tack a sailboat across the bay. Rather it was the incongruity of the people he was watching that irritated him: they were so totally out of place in such a resort at such a time.

Union leaders may score a proletarian point by convening in Scarborough or in Atlantic City in October. Clergymen may regard congregating in holiday camps in March as the twentieth-century equivalent of the hair shirt and derive solace therefrom. Politicians may kid their voters that they are working if they babble around tables in Brussels or Geneva at any time of year. But only scientists, their minds congested with calculus and their vision dimmed by nebulous theories, could possibly consider conducting ponderous arguments in Cannes at the end of May when the sun was bright but the temperature was at its most agreeable.

It must be admitted that the Saint had never had too high a regard for scientists as a breed. After all, he reflected, most of the really important things had been discovered by accident rather than through deliberate research. A watched kettle had boiled and heralded the Industrial Revolution, a forgotten fungus had provided penicillin, and a wine grower's mistake had produced cognac. The Saint sniffed the dark gold liquid in his glass as he raised it in silent salute to his ignorant benefactor, and waited for the comforting glow to diffuse through his body. On the whole, his summation went, the contributions of scientists to the health and creature comforts of mankind had been pretty well offset by the Pandora's boxload of death and destruction and pollution that they had also helped to let loose.

The era of the Saint's anonymity has already been mentioned. A scientist's evil discovery had been responsible, in an ultimate way, for bringing those golden days to a close, and for the death of one of the truest friends he would ever have.* Psychiatrists perhaps could have spent many happy hours pondering the significance of those events in his attitude to science and the irony of his present interest in it.

Soon the scientists would be gone and Cannes and the Palais would welcome arrivals more in keeping with their *raison d'être*. Hollywood had recently staged its seasonal corroboree, turning the town into a film fan's fantasy: starlets had enjoyed their exposure while photographers enjoyed the starlets, producers and directors had enjoyed talking about art while calculating how much their latest flick had grossed, gossip columnists had enjoyed one of the best junkets of the year, and everyone had gone home happy. Soon now the midsummer lemming swarm of traditional holiday-makers would be jostling each other for sweating room and paying exorbitantly for this privilege.

Anyone not knowing his identity might easily have thought him to be a leftover from the April Film Festival. The face was as tanned and handsome as any that ever appeared on the giant screen. The thick black hair swept straight back, the blue eyes that could be as warm as the Mediterranean or as cold as a Norwegian fjord, and the strength of the finely cut features, would have found him a place on any casting director's list. The sub-

* See *The Saint Closes the Case.*

tle difference was that in him it was not type casting: it was the real thing.

Among the throng on the sidewalk the Saint spotted Emma Maclett approaching. Even in a crowd twice as dense as that now perambulating the Croisette it would have been difficult to miss her. She was tall and slim and she moved with a weightless grace, her feet hardly seeming to touch the ground as she walked. Peat-brown hair curled just past her shoulders, green eyes flashing beneath a fringe. There was a mysterious, almost elfin air about her that was testimony to her Celtic ancestors. As she drew nearer, Simon recognised again the mixture of strength and innocence that had so attracted him at their first meeting.

The Saint's notoriety was such that it ensured him a steady flow of visitors to his door. Most of them wanted to enlist his services for something and Emma Maclett had been no exception. He had succumbed to the shy forthrightness of her by asking her in and inviting her to tell him her problem. It had been a dull day in a dull week and on such occasions the Saint would have been prepared to have been bored by someone far less attractive.

In the end her story had turned out to be far from tedious. Her father was Professor Andrew Maclett, a physicist. Did the Saint know much about science?

Simon had admitted that his scientific qualifications could be written on a postcard and still leave room for the address.

"But you have heard of solar energy?"

"Trapping the sun's rays to provide heat."

"That's the principle. Using the sun's energy obviously has tremendous potential. It's free and there's an unlimited supply. There are already houses which are heated by solar panels in the roof, but that's only scratching the surface. Lighting and heating a house is one thing, developing the technology to light and heat a town is another. That's what my father has done. The application of his process means that we could harness enough of the sun's energy to operate a full-sized power station. Think of it—free energy, no more reliance on oil or coal that are someday going to run out, with none of the dangers of nuclear power."

"I'd say that beats hanging around the local pub every afternoon. So what is your father's problem?"

"Free energy is fine in theory, but it also means a lot of trouble, and a gigantic loss for a great many people—oil companies, ancillary industries who rely on them, governments, trade unions—and they are only the major ones. My father has been officially told to shelve his plans. Not in the public interest! How on earth can they say that?"

"I take it Daddy has no intention of buttoning up."

"If you knew my father you wouldn't even ask. This is his life's work. Because he has insisted on carrying on with it, he was sacked from his chair at the university, and also lost the government grant that was paying for the research. He can't say anything publicly in Britain but he is to be the principal speaker at an energy conference in Cannes, and he intends taking the opportunity to tell the world. I'm scared they'll try to stop him. Also he's already turned down offers from the Soviets, who want the process for themselves, and I'm frightened they won't take no for an answer."

"And you want me to tag along and keep an eye on him?"

"That's right, just until after his speech. He's very independent, he'd never agree to the idea, so we can't tell him. You would somehow have to do it without his knowing."

Simon had looked out at the drizzle falling from a stone-grey sky. Something only he saw there amused him, and he smiled.

"I'm free at the moment, and the Riviera looks an increasingly inviting alternative to London in which to expend some energy."

And so it had been decided.

Simon caught the eye of his waiter, and made the international sign-language symbol of asking for his bill, holding up a flat-open left hand and miming the act of writing on it with his right. He rose as Emma reached the table and sat down.

After glancing cautiously each way she leaned across the table and whispered: "What have you found out?"

The Saint copied her actions, adding an exaggerated search under the table, and whispered: "Nothing."

The girl looked into two mocking blue eyes that dispelled the send-up before it could offend. Simon sat back in his chair and finished his cognac.

"I've been here three days and I'm three thousand francs up at the casino, but of villains I have seen neither hide nor hair."

Emma frowned.

"Then you think I was overreacting?"

"I didn't say that. I haven't found anything because I don't know what I'm looking for. There are thousands of people in Cannes, and any of them could be a prospective kidnapper or assassin. It's harder than looking for a needle in a haystack because at least you know what a needle looks like before you start."

Emma's face brightened.

"You're not giving up, then?"

Simon looked shocked.

"Certainly not. I've no intention of wasting the time I've spent on this jaunt so far. But if I can't go to the ungodly because I don't know who they are, then they will have to come to me because they do know who I am, or think they do . . . This must be your father now."

Emma turned her head to watch as a taxi stopped outside the Palais and her father emerged. To the casual observer the Saint would have appeared to be looking directly at his companion but he had carefully placed his chair so that he could see without being seen to be watching. It was the first time he had viewed the professor except from photographs, and he liked what he saw.

Maclett stood a head above the tallest of the welcoming

committee, and looked as if he had been hewn from a Highland hillside. His shoulders strained against the confines of a check tweed sports jacket, a mop of reddish hair that hadn't seen a brush since breakfast framed a strong, confident face that should have belonged to a trawler skipper or an oil prospector rather than to a physicist. The Saint could picture him wearing a kilt and wielding a claymore, and instantly believed his daughter's account of his temper.

The introductions over, the party was mounting the steps.

"Who is he?" asked the Saint, indicating the little goateed man who led the way.

"Dr. Francis Riguard. He's the president of the institute and the chairman of the conference."

As the group disappeared inside the building, Emma turned back to the table to see the Saint vigorously tousling his hair.

"What are you doing?"

"I am engaged in practising the art of disguise, or rather creating a personality. It is a common myth that to change your appearance you have to hide behind a hedge of false hair, puff the cheeks out with rubber pads, and apply a coating of plaster calculated to result in you looking like a make-up artist's conception of the Thing From The Pit. In fact, all that is necessary is to adopt an identity. In this case, the angry young scientist."

As he spoke, the Saint placed a row of cheap pens in the breast pocket of his jacket; a crumpled tie was knotted loosely around the unbuttoned collar of his shirt, and a pair of heavy black-rimmed spectacles rested earnestly on the bridge of his nose. Finally he went down and retrieved a bulging manila folder from beneath the table.

In less time than it took him to explain his activities, the elegant tourist who would have had the doors of any casino on the coast immediately opened for him was replaced by a harassed understrapper who would have gone unnoticed in any important office.

The girl watched the transformation, wondering if the man

she had entrusted with her father's protection had been affected by his luncheon lubricants.

"And the file?" she asked at last, because she felt she had to say something.

"Ah, that's the *pièce de résistance!* It is my belief that you can walk into any official building anywhere in the world so long as you carry a file and look as if you know where you're going. A clipboard is better, but I couldn't get hold of one. A man carrying a briefcase will be searched, but there is something inherently innocent about a man with a folder of papers. This one contains a copy of *Paris-Match,* yesterday's *Figaro,* and half a ream of hotel notepaper."

The Saint spread folding money on the bill which had been placed before him, and stood up.

"I'm going to work. You can watch if you like, but don't show that you know me. I'll see you back at the hotel in an hour."

2

Head bowed, arms protectively cradling the file of papers, the Saint trotted up the steps and in through the main doors of the Palais without earning a second glance from the attendants standing by them. Once inside he stood for a moment to gain his bearings and savour the welcoming coolness of the foyer before following the signs directing him to the hall where the official opening ceremony was taking place.

The two men standing on either side of the salle entrance wore no uniforms but there was an impressive breadth to their shoulders and an alertness in their eyes that told the Saint they would not be so easily fooled as their colleagues outside. He left the file on a window ledge and pretended to be studying a noticeboard on the opposite side of the foyer.

Through the glazed doors he could see Riguard standing on

the stage at the far end of the auditorium. Those scheduled to be the principal speakers at the conference were ranged on both sides of him with Maclett in the place of honour on his right.

With no apparent haste the Saint neared the doors. As he did so the chairman's words became clearer:

". . . And the great event of the week will, of course, be the lecture by our honoured guest, Professor Maclett, on some of the implications of his spectacular breakthrough in the field of solar energy . . ."

The cue was too apt for a person with Simon Templar's sense of the dramatic to miss. It came as he drew level with the double doors, and he moved with the speed of a panther. He took two steps to his right and launched himself into a charge, hitting the centre of the doors with his shoulder. Before the first steward had begun to react he was standing in the middle of the main aisle, his voice raised in impassioned protest.

"His breakthrough! It wasn't his breakthrough, it's mine! I was his research student at Cambridge. The great Professor Maclett stole it from me. The man's a thief and a liar!"

The stewards were quick to recover. Grabbing Simon by the arms, they prepared to drag him away. The Saint's biceps tensed instinctively at the contact, and for an instant the two men paused, surprised by the muscle beneath their fingers. Simon took advantage of the delay to fire his next salvo.

"He put me off it, told me it was rubbish—now he announces it as his own! He stole it, I tell you!"

The spectators were torn between watching the antics of the raving protester halfway down the aisle and the spectacle being provided by Maclett. At the Saint's first words the professor stood up, rage quickly taking the place of astonishment as the allegations registered. His face had turned an interesting shade that was a mixture of dark red and bright purple; his hands clenched into fists, and he began to climb down from the stage.

The possibility of a physical brawl with the man he was supposed to be protecting had not figured in Simon's plan of campaign. His muscles relaxed.

"OK, boys, take me away," he whispered to the men trying to do just that, and as they roughly obliged he managed one final shout at the lumbering professor and his goggle-eyed audience.

"He's a fraud and a thief!"

Once away from the auditorium, the stewards made it clear that they planned to conclude their work with an airborne descent of the steps outside the Palais. The Saint had other ideas. He stopped. The stewards, finding their acquiescent charge suddenly as immobile as an oak, had no option but to do the same. They looked at each other and then at the Saint, who by that time should have been picking himself up off the sidewalk. Simon's fingers closed around the wrists of the hands holding him with the strength of a bear trap snapping shut and removed them from his person.

He smiled.

"Don't bother. I'll see myself out."

A few curious passers-by had gathered, and the Saint was eager to vacate the scene before the possible arrival of the Law. An empty taxi was stalled in the intermittent traffic jam outside, and Simon opened the rear door and slid in behind the driver.

"Hôtel Bellevue, please."

The driver nodded and re-engaged the gears. He was small and slightly built and out of proportion to the spacious white Buick he drove. His skin was tanned the color of old mahogany, he wore a black waist-length zipper jacket over a casual shirt of eye-searing hues and shapeless blue jeans met equally ancient blue sneakers.

As he eased the big car into the flow of traffic the Saint looked back in time to see a dark blue Mercedes pull out of the line of parked cars behind and swing in behind them. Simon leaned forward and spoke in fluent French.

"Drive to the station, then up the Boulevard Carnot, then turn back towards the Croisette by the Boulevard d'Alsace. I would like to arrive at the hotel from the other side."

The driver nodded his acceptance of each eccentric direction without argument, as if being asked to drive three times the necessary distance was an everyday event. Once his eyes met the Saint's as both glanced in the rear-view mirror at the same time. What might have been a smile hovered at the corners of his mouth. He raised his hand and adjusted the glass a few degrees.

"Like that, you will see better," was his only comment.

The Saint laughed.

"Yes, that is much better. Thank you."

The driver shrugged, as if to say that it was quite usual for him to have passengers who thought they were being followed.

As he turned the car into the Boulevard d'Alsace, he asked: "The Mercedes, you want me to lose it?"

Simon shook his head.

"No, thank you. I wish to know who is in it, not get away from them, once I am sure they are on our trail."

It was an admission that could have proved foolish but the Saint had the gift of being able to judge the characters of others after the briefest of encounters, and his intuition told him the driver was not only likely to be discreet but might be able to offer real help if trusted.

When they eventually reached the hotel Simon was pleased to see the Mercedes still the same distance behind. He climbed out slowly, to give his shadow time to find a parking place, and added a generous tip to the already exorbitant fare.

"Merci, m'sieu."

"Merci à vous. Tell me, do you have a regular base, or do you cruise around looking for passengers?"

The driver pointed to the hotel.

"This is my base."

The Saint smiled.

"*Très bien.* We shall probably be seeing more of each other."

The driver made a sweeping gesture with his hand. "Just ask for Gaby. Everyone knows Gaby, and I know everyone."

"*Alors, à bientôt,*" the Saint promised, and with a wave turned and entered the hotel.

The Bellevue was a new hotel that was distinguished only by its technological amenities and total lack of character. It was part of an international chain in which each link was identical, so that once inside the door the guest could not be certain whether he was in Bombay or Buenos Aires. It had all the intimacy of an airport lounge, and the welcoming friendliness of a police station charge room. It was the last sort of hotel in which any of the Saint's friends would have expected to find him, which was exactly why he was staying there on this occasion.

In the reflection of the glass doors he watched the driver of the Mercedes crossing from the parking area. Simon placed him in the pigeonhole the gossip writers label "playboy." He matched the Saint for height and build and carried himself with an arrogance that showed he was accustomed to being looked at and admired. He affected a blue blazer and immaculate white slacks and was handsome in the smooth way that appeals to middle-aged countesses and wealthy widows.

The concierge looked up and smiled as the Saint approached his counter. Simon had a fleeting vision of the same man smiling the same smile behind the same desk in a dozen countries simultaneously.

"Sebastian Tombs. Room 309. Have there been any messages for me?" The Saint's voice was deliberately clear, and he knew it would carry to the bookstall where his shadow was intent on studying the front page of the *Herald Tribune*.

The concierge took down his room key, checked the box under it, and informed Simon that no one had called. The Saint thanked him, and on looking around saw that the bookstall was deserted.

Once in his room, he barely had time to change his clothes and pour a small dose from the duty-free bottle he had brought from London Airport onto a pile of crushed ice before Emma knocked. He opened the door with one hand and proffered the drink with the other.

Emma accepted the glass with a smile.

"Thank you. That was quite a performance you staged this afternoon."

Simon provisioned another glass and led the way out to the balcony.

"I must say I thought I caught the tone rather well," he admitted modestly.

For a few moments both were silent as they tasted their drinks and gazed out across the rooftops to the sea.

"Do you think it will do any good?"

The Saint shifted his chair to get the maximum benefit from the breeze that was beginning to drift shorewards.

"It already has."

He recounted the drive back to the hotel and described the man in the Mercedes.

Emma thought for a while but finally shook her head.

"I don't know him, so he certainly isn't anything to do with the conference, not officially anyway. But how do you know he was following you? He could simply have been coming to the hotel."

"He would hardly have taken the route I chose, and he left in a hurry as soon as he had found out my name—to report back, I suppose. The question is—to whom?"

He was about to put forward some of the possible answers to that problem when a violent hammering on the door made further conversation impossible. The Saint put on his glasses and stood up. He pointed Emma towards the bathroom door: "In there, and stay quiet."

The girl hesitated.

"What if it's reporters who saw you at the conference?"

"Then they are going to have much better headlines if they find you in my room, so shoo."

The banging grew louder and Simon hurried to open the door before it broke under the strain.

The moment he slipped the catch, the door was sent crashing back against the wall, and without waiting to be invited Professor Maclett strode in, planting himself in the centre of the room, legs apart, arms folded across his chest, fingers twitching as he clutched the cloth of his jacket sleeves. He was obviously fighting to control his temper, and the Saint kept a prudent arm's length away in case he lost it.

"All right, young man, let's hear it! You pop up in the middle of a major conference, shouting I've stolen yer recipe. Before I rip yer liver out I'd like t'hear just exactly what y'think yer talking about."

The Saint raised two hands in a gesture of peace.

"Professor, I do understand you . . ."

"M'process is me own, and so's me honour, y'young pup. If ever in me life I've stole s'much as a dram from any man's locker I'll be having y'tell me so t'my face right here and now in private."

From the corner of his eye Simon saw the bathroom door open, and stood aside so that Maclett could see his daughter. A look of astonishment replaced the one of anger that had coloured the professor's face. Simon waved his hand between them.

"Professor Maclett, Miss Maclett. Miss Maclett, Professor Maclett."

Maclett turned on his daughter, ignoring the Saint.

"What the hell are you doing here, girl?"

"Employing me to watch you, I'm afraid," Simon explained. "Now that we all know each other, why don't we discuss this over a drink?"

But Maclett was not to be so easily pacified.

"I'll be taking no drinks with you, young man!"

Emma came between them, putting her hands on her father's shoulders, her voice softly scolding him.

"Now, Daddy, stop shouting. You know no one can understand that accent of yours when you start yelling."

"I was not yelling," Maclett yelled.

"You were yelling. Now why don't you take Simon's advice and go for a drink with him, it'll help you to calm down."

The big man visibly softened as he looked down into his daughter's eyes.

"Aye, I suppose I could do with a dram at that." He turned back to the Saint. "C'mon then, young man—but I warn ye, your story had better be a good one."

They rode down in silence and did not speak again until the drinks had been poured and they were seated in a corner of the hotel bar.

"Your daughter's simply afraid for you."

"Nonsense."

"And with good reason," Simon continued. "You're a very big fish with a very big secret."

Maclett smiled grimly, more to himself than to his companion.

"It won't be a secret for long. I came to this convention to make it so public they'll have to recognise it. Those big oil corporations and consortiums are always stuffing independent progress on the back shelf somewhere. Well, not in this case, I can tell y'. Not in this case."

"Yes, I can understand . . ." Simon began, but Maclett overrode him.

"Y'know how many life-giving breakthroughs get locked away in closets every year by the big-money fellas with their vested interests and their—"

The Saint could see the conversation becoming a somewhat

hackneyed diatribe on the evil machinations of big business, and cut in firmly.

"Professor, we were talking about your security."

"Look here, now, lad, right now I just want one thing—"

"I agree, another drink."

Simon signalled to the waiter to refill their glasses. While that was being done, he took the opportunity to put his case.

"Listen, Professor, I'm sorry about all the melodrama back in the conference hall, but at least now no one will accuse me of being concerned about your welfare."

Maclett downed half his second Scotch in one.

"Laddie, I tell you, and I'll tell that silly daughter of mine, I don't need t'be coddled. I haven't been doin' equations so long I can't still throw a good right hand, y'know."

"That I can believe."

"I swung a pickaxe for every minute o'physics they ever taught me."

Simon was not to be swayed, though he admitted that he would have welcomed Maclett on his side in a free-for-all.

"Emma's told me you've already turned away some tentative probes by the eastern bloc in the last year alone. You're valuable. They want you, and if they want you badly enough they'll keep trying to have you. One way or another."

Maclett chuckled at the vision conjured up by the Saint's words.

"Come on, laddie, what do you think they'd do—kidnap me?"

"It's possible."

"Once I announce th'application of m'theory, who th'devil's going to bother needing me then? M'daughter's a well-meanin' child and yer may be a well-meanin' man, but I haven't needed ye and I don't and I won't."

Maclett drained his glass and rose.

"I thank ye fer the drink, laddie, if fer nothin' else."

Simon watched the professor leave and decided to follow his

example. He was rapidly tiring of being cooped up in conference halls and hotels, and the prospect of a stroll by the sea in some fresh air was inviting. Besides which, it would give him an opportunity to assess how the Ungodly's interest in him was developing. He paid for the drinks and sauntered through the foyer and out into the afternoon sunshine.

He paid no attention to the young man leaning against one of the pillars supporting the hotel portico, or to the black Renault that just stopped in the centre of the car park until he felt something hard jab into the hollow of his spine. The voice in his ear was low but firm.

"There's a car over there. Why don't you step into it?"

3

The Saint turned his head and appraised the bulge in the speaker's pocket with an expert eye, but he did not move. He was annoyed at having been caught so easily and had no intention of further damaging his record by instantly obeying the order. His eyes travelled the length of the young man who stood slightly behind him, subjecting him to a silent, mocking evaluation. They started with the suede slip-ons, journeyed up the slightly rumpled trousers of the light grey suit, lingered for a moment on the stainless steel watch bracelet that showed on the left wrist and the heavy heraldic ring on the third finger of the one square hand that was visible to him, took in the thick set of the shoulders, and finished on the freshly scrubbed face. His nostrils registered the assault of a lavishly applied cheap aftershave.

This was not the playboy type of the Mercedes, but one of an outwardly tougher class, or consciously trying to give that impression. The voice was public-school English moderated by an affected mid-Atlantic drawl. There was a tenseness to the features and a flicker behind the eyes that told him the young man might act rashly if his ego was scratched.

Simon caught the other's tone perfectly.

"I believe I'll do just what you suggest."

The young man's eyes narrowed at the mimicry and he pushed the gun viciously into the Saint's back.

"Move!"

The Saint strolled leisurely across to the Renault, which was parked a few yards away from Gaby's taxi. The cab driver was sitting in the front passenger seat, contriving to read a newspaper while keeping his eyes switching to a look-out for possible customers. As he saw the Saint approaching, the newspaper disappeared and he was standing outside with the rear door open by the time Simon drew level.

Simon registered regret by spreading out his hands and shaking his head.

"Not now, Gaby, *mon vieux*. This gentleman insists on showing me the sights himself."

Another forceful prod in his ribs told him to keep moving, and the Saint obeyed it. He caught the puzzled look in Gaby's eyes, and knew that the significance of the situation had not escaped him.

Simon got in beside the driver, who reached over to open the door, and the young man climbed in the back, sitting directly behind him. The Saint settled himself comfortably in his seat, stretching out his legs and resting his feet on a small fire extinguisher clipped to the side of the car under the dashboard. The driver, a sallow, hound-faced type with a droopy moustache, looked at neither of them, but simply took his foot off the brake and sent them skidding out of the hotel grounds to the sound of protesting rubber. In the wing mirror Simon could see the white Buick a half-dozen car lengths behind.

"Don't you think you should introduce yourselves?" said the Saint, "I'd like to have something to call you, beside the rude names that my grandmother always told me never to use."

"Shut up."

Simon detected the first sign of strain in the young man's voice, and he smiled. The driver showed no emotion at all but looked only at the road ahead, his whole concentration devoted to his piloting.

The Saint turned to his captor.

"Wherever we're going, is it far?"

He was met with a silent stare. Simon nodded understandingly.

"I suppose they only program you for specific tasks." An idea seemed to strike him. "Of course, that's it, you're really mobile computers, and you're going to be the star turn at the science conference, but someone let you out by mistake, and you're wearing that aftershave to mask the smell of oil."

A red glow was creeping up the young man's neck.

"Shut up and turn around. Any more cracks, and you'll arrive with a lump on your head."

The Saint shrugged, and resumed his former position. His feet tested the spring bracket holding the extinquisher and he spent the next few minutes calculating angles and distances. This task completed, he settled back to enjoy the ride.

They had zigzagged through on to the main road out of town westwards towards Antibes, but now immediately took a minor side road on the left that wound steeply up into the landscaped terraces of the snob residential section known idolatrously as La Californie. From the car, there were occasional backward glimpses of the sea shimmering in the summer warmth, but the best views were reserved to the expensive properties set back from the road, most of which were established before the upper classes had accepted the practice of sea bathing. To an unobservant observer, Simon Templar might have seemed to have fallen half asleep, his body relaxed, his eyes half closed against the sun's glare. The driver's concentration was completely absorbed by the intricate windings of the road, and his colleague was looking out of the side windows in obvious confidence in his control of the situation. The Saint knew that if he was to make a move it would have to be soon.

He slid the toe of his right shoe under the fire extinguisher and flicked the release catch with his left, sending the cylinder spinning towards him. He caught it on the half turn and smashed down the handle as he completed the maneuver, directing the jet of foam straight into the face of the gun-toter behind him. Suddenly blinded, the victim shot his hands to his eyes as the Saint dived across the back of his seat, one hand reaching for the young man's gun, the other flinging the spurting extinguisher into the clean-scrubbed face.

The driver had stamped on the brake as soon as the commotion started, but he was too busy trying to control the resultant skidding to offer any resistance, and too sensible to do anything but leave his hands on the wheel once the motor had stopped. Simon turned to him.

"Now be a nice boy and give us your toy." Simon took the gun from under the driver's armpit and considered the relative merits of the arsenal he had collected. The first was a nickel-plated .22 that, although deadly enough at close range, was more suited to a lady's handbag. The Saint tossed it out of the window and retained the heavier army issue .38 automatic which the aftershave advertisement had provided. He turned off the engine and pocketed the ignition keys before getting out of the car and opening the rear door.

"Out."

The junior kidnapper stumbled out, still trying to clear the foam from his eyes. Simon pushed him into the front passenger seat, got into the back, and returned the keys to the driver.

"Don't think I don't want to go wherever you were going," he said. "I just don't like being crowded. Now just carry on as if I hadn't interrupted."

The Saint waved an arm out of the window as a sign to Gaby, who had stopped his taxi a safe twenty metres behind to follow.

As impassive as before, the hound-faced driver steered the car only a little farther along a high grey stone wall, following its contours until they led to an impressive arched gateway, into which he turned.

Carefully manicured lawns, dotted here and there with geometric flower beds and sculptured bushes, ran down to the drive that curved its way up to the front of a long, low, whitewashed villa that spread itself across a terrace cut into the hillside. Set to one side of the building, in a southern-exposed alcove, was an oval swimming pool. Roman-style mosaics were set into the marble surround; towering columns, entwined with vines and interspersed with classical statues of satyrs and nymphs, embraced a scene that could have come straight from a Hollywood set for a period spectacle.

In perfect harmony with the decor, there seemed to be girls everywhere, walking across the grass verges, swimming in the pool, or sunbathing beside it. And watching them like some Roman emperor was Sir William Curdon.

The Saint recognised him at once.

His heavy frame filled the thronelike chair he sat in, a Montecristo cigar in one hand and a champagne glass in the other, and he looked very much the part. He watched as the car stopped in front of the villa and the Saint shepherded his charges across the drive.

Curdon's grey eyes were as revealing as a sea fog. A girl swam to the edge of the pool, and he put down his cigar and glass and obligingly poured champagne into her waiting mouth, while his free hand slid under the cushion at his side and clicked off the safety catch of an automatic.

The two kidnappers turned hostages followed the movement of the Saint's gun barrel, and moved to one side to allow Curdon and the Saint an uninterrupted view of each other.

Simon smiled his most Saintly smile, but his eyes never strayed from the scene, keeping all three males within his field of vision, and paying particular attention to the cushion that Curdon's hand rested on.

"You sent for me, did you, chum? I must say, the Secret Service are living well these days. I thought that was only in the movies."

Curdon ignored him, turning instead to the executive kidnapper who was shifting his weight uneasily from one foot to the other. The effort Curdon was making to remain calm showed in the grating of his voice.

"Cartwright, I do not expect to have my operatives brought back to me as the prisoners of those they were sent to bring in."

The Saint nodded understandingly.

"Oh, I do know how you feel, Willie. But don't blame yourself. So hard to get reliable help these days. Even D16 evidently has to take what it can get."

Curdon's control cracked at last, and he shouted at the hapless aide: "Tell me, Cartwright, just who do you suppose this person to be?"

The mid-Atlantic drawl disappeared, making Cartwright sound like a truant offering excuses to his housemaster.

"It's Sebastian Tombs, sir. The man who threatened Professor Maclett at the conference."

Curdon's eyes closed as if in pain. When he opened them again they were fixed on the Saint.

"All right, Templar, what's your play in this game?"

Simon used a free hand to pour himself a glass of champagne which he raised in a mocking toast.

"Emma Maclett was worried about her father. She asked me to look after him."

"Calling him a fraud in public is an odd way of doing that."

"Oh really, Willie! It's ploy number three in your beginner's manual." Simon paused. "You are past that by now, I hope."

"Looking after Professor Maclett happens to be my department's job."

"Perhaps if you'd let Emma Maclett know that, she wouldn't have felt she needed me." The Saint looked at Cartwright and the Renault driver, and sighed. "Or maybe she would have felt she needed me. Mind you, I couldn't do my protesting half as handsomely."

"This villa belongs to a rich cousin of mine. Sells swamp land in Florida."

"And the girls?"

"He's very selective about his staff."

"So I can see. Two redheads, two blondes, two brunettes. Just like the civil service, everything in duplicate."

Sir William Curdon's tone was defensive, almost apologetic.

"One gets a bit sick of being considered disqualified from living because one happens to work for the government. The only thing the department's paying for is the champagne, and even that's non-vintage."

"I don't know how you manage."

The rage that was bubbling near the surface finally boiled over as the Saint had expected it would.

"I don't like you, Templar. I don't like your attitude to authority. I don't like your meddling in the affairs of the Service. Most of all, I don't trust your motives in this affair. I'm warning you, put one foot wrong and I'll have it nailed to the floor."

"Better do it yourself, then," the Saint replied coolly, and jerked his thumb at Cartwright. "This one'd probably hit his own thumb. By the way, how did your bloodhounds find me?"

"Cartwright was at the conference and he followed you back to the hotel."

Simon shook his head at his own shortcoming in having only looked for one tail. Cartwright must have been behind the Mercedes all the time. He helped himself to a cigar from the box on the table and smiled.

"It's been a pleasure meeting you again, Willie. But next time you want a chat, you needn't send the strong-arm squad. Just call me."

He turned to go, and saw Cartwright's foot move as he passed. Not wishing to pass up such an excuse, he allowed himself to be partly tripped, and stumbled forward without going down.

"How are you without a fire extinguisher?" Cartwright asked, with some of his former cockiness.

The Saint turned back, straightening as he did so. His left hand pushed his glasses back onto the bridge of his nose as his right streaked out a stiff-fingered thrust into the gap at the base of Cartwright's ribs. The man folded backwards onto the sun lounger. The Saint casually swung his foot and tipped it into the pool. Cartwright disappeared beneath the water, and Simon waited for him to surface before replying to his question.

"Oh, I get by."

He removed the clip from the automatic and tossed it into the pool beside Cartwright.

"You shouldn't give the children toys like that, Willie—they're dangerous."

Gaby had parked his cab behind the Renault, and the Saint climbed in beside him.

"You're beginning to grow on me, Gaby."

Simon handed him Curdon's cigar. The driver accepted it, sniffed it, and put it in his mouth, but made no move to light it.

"I saw what happened outside the hotel," was the brief explanation he offered as he sent the car speeding back towards Cannes.

"But how did you know I was not being arrested? That those men were not the police?"

"I know the police in Cannes—and they know me."

Simon decided it was politic not to enquire too deeply into their relationship. He lapsed into silence as he considered Curdon's involvement and how it might affect his own plans for Maclett's safety.

Presently Gaby said: "The man in the Mercedes, his name is Jacques Demmell."

"How do you know that?"

The Saint did not try to hide his surprise and Gaby's face split in a rare grin.

"I recognised the car. It belongs to a hire company I used to drive for, so I made enquiries."

"Anything besides the name?"

"Not a great deal. He often comes here during the season. He has a reputation as a friend of lonely ladies, especially the rich kind. He has a flat in the town but he's been spending most of his time on a yacht called *Protégé*. It is moored in the Port Canto."

"Yes, I've seen it. Is it his?"

"No, it belongs to a woman, and believe me she is quite a woman." Gaby raised one hand from the wheel long enough to draw a curving outline in the air. "Not the usual type of woman he attracts."

The Mercedes was parked outside the hotel when they returned. Simon touched the grill; the engine was cold. There was no sign of Demmell in the lounges and bars, and the Saint was thoughtful as he prudently rode the elevator up to the floor immediately above his own, and walked back down the stairs to his floor.

4

The Saint passed silently along the corridor and stood motionless outside his room, his ears straining to identify the muffled sounds that reached him through the door and to fix in his mind the exact location of his uninvited guest. He took the key from his pocket, but before he could move, a room service waiter clattered around the corner pushing a trolley, and immediately the noises ceased. The Saint cursed the unsuspecting man all the way into the elevator.

Simon stood with his back pressed against the wall, fitting

his key into the spring lock with the tips of his fingers, and sent the door crashing inwards the instant the catch was released. He entered the room with a fluid sidestep that removed him from the line of fire, registering the chaos of his surroundings in a single sweeping glance as he swivelled in a half crouch towards the space behind the slowly closing door.

The edge of the door had caught Demmell near the middle of the face, splitting his nose and lip. A workmanlike .44 Bulldog revolver was held across his body and had he been blessed with faster reflexes he might have followed Bob Ford into the ranks of those who have written finis to the careers of the greatest outlaws of their age, but the Saint gave him no time to achieve such distinction. As Simon turned, pivoting on the ball of his right foot, his left came up in a swinging arc that smashed into Demmell's gun hand with the speed and force of an unleashed flail. The revolver spun from Demmell's suddenly lifeless fingers, and he cried out as the searing pain ripped through his arm.

The Saint straightened, and took in the upheaval around him in greater detail. Drawers had been pulled out and their contents spilled onto the floor, his suitcase had been upturned and the few things he had left in it scattered around the room; cushions, pictures, books, ornaments, anything that could conceivably serve as a hiding place had been pulled apart.

The scene angered him not so much because of its untidiness as because it bore all the hallmarks of the amateur, and the Saint disliked dealing with amateurs. Searching a room is both an art and a science. It calls for a lightness of touch, a photographic memory, and the ability to analyse the psychology of the occupier to determine where the objects of the search are most likely to be hidden. An experienced professional investigator will turn over a room, miss nothing, and leave it as tidy as when he entered, aware that the extra care taken will give a valuable margin of time before his intrusion is discovered. Should he not find what he is looking for, he knows that by not making his visit obvious he has left open the probability for a return call. The amateur, on the other hand, blunders about, not only making life more difficult for himself but also causing unnecessary distress to the victim of his attention.

"The maid service here has just gone to hell," Simon observed, as he picked up a favourite sports jacket and replaced it carefully on its hanger.

He had shown his contempt for Demmell by almost turning his back on him. The revolver still lay in the centre of the room, an equal distance from both of them. Demmell saw his chance and took it, as the Saint had expected him to.

The man moved with creditable speed, but he had covered only half the distance before a strange medley of sensations overwhelmed him. One moment he was in the middle of a diving roll, fingers outstretched towards the butt of the gun; the next, he met an irresistible force coming in the opposite direction with the speed of an express train: for one transfixed instant he felt himself flying backwards, and then the wall hit him and he sank to his knees, with a sickening breathless agony in his stomach eclipsing the pain in his arm.

Simon's heel came gently to rest and he turned to face the retching man now climbing groggily back to the vertical.

The Saint's voice was a mocking drawl: "Enough?"

In answer Demmell catapulted himself off the wall, his shoulder catching Simon in the chest and the momentum sending them both crashing to the floor. The Saint was impressed. He had kicked men in that way before, and they had rarely risen so quickly. It boded well for Demmell's fitness and the exercise still to come.

Just as his back touched the floor the Saint twisted his whole body, sending them both rolling over. His fist shot upwards towards the other's head in a vicious right hook that should have ended the fight, but the blow never connected. Demmell broke its force with his arm and his heel whipped backwards to explode at the base of the Saint's spine.

The Saint's body arched like a bow and a freezing numbness seemed to grip every muscle. He relaxed his grip and Demmell wriggled free, aiming a kick at the Saint's head as he rose. Instinctively Simon's arms crossed to block the blow, and he rolled away from his opponent and pulled himself to his feet with an effort that was more mental than physical.

Demmell was grinning as he waded in for the next round, and Simon returned his smile. The numbness was passing, to be replaced by the invigorating glow of pumping adrenalin.

Demmell's arm sped from his shoulder in a straight karate punch to the Saint's temples. Simon fended it easily with his forearm and replied with a slashing chop to the ribs. Demmell grunted and stepped back, lashing out with a wild kick as he did so. Simon sidestepped and caught the heel of the other's shoe as it completed its trajectory. For an instant their eyes locked, and for the first time Simon saw fear on his antagonist's face. The Saint smiled, and pulled.

Demmell fell heavily, and the Saint, keeping hold of the foot, followed him down, twisting the heel and toe as he went. Demmell's body jackknifed. His hands reached forward to take the strain off his buckled leg, and the Saint's fist hit him flush on the side of the face, sending his head banging back to the floor. Simon rested his weight on Demmell's ribs, forcing the air from his body. He released the foot with a final excruciating wrench, and his forearm descended like a guillotine on the other's throat.

Simon grinned into Demmell's bulging eyes, lifting the pressure of his forearm slightly to allow the passage of a modicum of air. His voice was hard and low.

"Question time."

Perhaps it was something in Demmell's expression, some spark of hope lighting his eyes, perhaps it was a sixth sense awakening too late to be helpful, but suddenly Simon knew that he hadn't won. Instinct told him to turn, but there was no time to obey before the blow fell. Constellations spun in front of him, and long before his body collapsed all consciousness had gone and he was free-falling into oblivion.

5

Gradually the darkness lightened.

The Saint lay perfectly still. Someone appeared to be hammering nails into the base of his skull. He was aware that he was lying on his back, with something soft beneath his head. His senses were stirred by two separate sensations that managed to filter through the haze enveloping his brain. A delicate aroma of expensive perfume was wafting across his face, and his taste buds were approving the smoothness of the champagne that was being gently trickled into his mouth.

Full consciousness returned, but he delayed opening his eyes for fear that the vision the two sensations conjured up would be dispersed by reality.

"Bollinger, I believe."

"Nothing but the best."

The voice was soft and low, containing the tantalising hint of an accent he could not readily identify. He could feel the lips that framed the words almost caressing his ear. He opened one eye and then the other, to focus on the face above.

Sapphire blue eyes sparkled from flawless tanned skin, the full lips were slightly parted, and the vision was framed by cascading flaxen hair that caught and trapped the sun like a halo.

Simon shook his head, closed his eyes and opened them again but the vision remained. He levered himself into a sitting position, wincing at the pain in his neck and back.

"I've heard of ministering angels--but champagne?"

The vision poured out a glass and handed it to him. "For the fevered brow, it's the only thing."

The Saint rubbed his neck.

"How is it for the fevered neck?"

"Best applied internally."

The vision held out her hand and helped Simon to his feet. The Saint's eyes narrowed fractionally as he felt the strength of the fingers and the bone-hard skin along the edge of the palm, but he was too intent on absorbing the rest of the picture to pay immediate attention to either.

The vision smoothed the front of a white cotton dress that appeared to consist of little except a neckline and a hem. Nature had been generous with her gifts, and Simon agreed it would have been ungracious to hide them.

The girl raised her glass.

"Cheers, I'm Samantha Lord."

Simon returned the gesture.

"Sebastian Tombs."

He rested on the arm of a chair and Samantha sat opposite him, one seemingly endless leg crossed over the other. She took a slim platinum case from her bag and proffered a cigaret. He shook his head.

"No longer one of my vices."

"Well, perhaps it leaves you more energy for your remaining ones." Samantha selected a cigaret, lit it, and watched the exhaled smoke rise towards the ceiling until it finally disappeared.

Her gaze travelled slowly round the room.

"You must have had an untidy upbringing."

"I mislaid a cufflink."

Samantha leaned forward and removed his glasses. "Maybe you'd have a better chance of finding it without those."

He decided for the moment not to confirm or deny her apparent diagnosis of his natural vision.

"Where did you spring from anyway?"

"I have a suite on this floor. I'd just come in to get something, and when I passed your room the door was open and I saw you. I never could resist a gentleman in distress."

Samantha had stood up as she talked, and the Saint also

rose, taking her empty champagne glass and placing it alongside his own on the table.

"What makes you think I'm a gentleman?"

His hands rested on her shoulders, and her mouth opened as he moved closer. Their eyes held each other's as their lips met.

The crash of the door being slammed shattered the spell. Emma Maclett walked purposefully into the room, ignored Samantha, and spoke directly to the Saint.

"Hi! I'm from the *Herald Tribune*."

Samantha's voice was as sweet as vinegar.

"Cancel my subscription."

The Saint stepped out of the line of fire, assuming the professional indifference of a tennis umpire.

Emma's green eyes flashed.

"I do hope I'm breaking something up."

Samantha looked at the Saint inquiringly.

"Sweet thing. Your aunt?"

"I'm just a local science correspondent."

Samantha shrugged.

"Well, I wouldn't want to stand here in the way of a Nobel Prize."

The Saint, fearing a full-scale battle, stepped between them.

"Sam, I really don't know how to thank you."

Emma's eyes flashed.

"I thought you were doing that when I walked in."

Samantha spared her a long, withering look.

"Bitterness is a terrible thing, dear," she cautioned, and turned back to the Saint. "I'm very easy to thank. Just take me to dinner tonight."

"I'd love to. Where can I find you?"

"The lobby, eight sharp."

"Till tonight then."

Samantha turned as she reached the door, and winked at the Saint.

"Help yourselves to the champagne, it can brighten up the dullest occasion."

After the door closed, Emma still could not hide her jealousy. "Who was she—your leg man?"

"I found some eager character ransacking my room. I was about to ask him some questions when I was knocked out. She revived me."

"That part I saw. And while you were out, my father also went out."

"Where? With whom?"

"To see someone called Curdon. He wouldn't tell me any more."

The Saint relaxed.

"It's all right. Curdon is a section head with D16. He's here to look out for your father too."

"D16! But why didn't he tell me he already had protection?"

"I don't know, just as I don't know why our recently departed vision of loveliness should knock me out and then revive me."

"She knocked you out!"

"I didn't actually see who it was, but she said she was passing and just happened to glance in, not very easy considering the door was shut. Also she has hard hands, the kind of hardness that comes from practising karate by demolishing the odd housebrick, and the blow that laid me out was as expertly delivered a karate chop as it has ever been my misfortune to receive."

"But you're still going to meet her tonight."

"Of course. How else can I find out what game she's playing? Now I've got a room to clear up and a shower to take. I'm interviewing for chambermaids and backscrubbers, if you'd like to apply."

"It's a tempting offer, but I've had better. I'll keep in touch."

Simon escorted her to the elevator and returned to repair the havoc in his room. When most of the mess had been straightened out he showered, the needle-thin jets of cold water stinging and revitalising his body. He dressed in a lightweight jacket and slacks and carefully combed his hair back into place. Anyone witnessing his actions would have found it difficult to believe that less than an hour before he had been fighting for his life, and even to the Saint the memory of his clash with Demmell was rapidly fading. There were too few minutes in any day to spend even one of them thinking about what might have been.

He left the hotel by a back door and cut quickly through a side street until he reached the Croisette. He crossed to the sidewalk on the shore side and headed towards the Palm Beach Casino. There was still an hour to go before he was due to meet Samantha, and he hoped to enjoy some fresh air and leisurely exercise.

The town seemed to hang in limbo, a no-man's-time, a long pause in which to reflect or prepare. The beach was deserted except for a handful of diehard sunworshippers soaking up the last rays. In the sidewalk bars and restaurants, waiters were sweeping and laying tables in readiness for the evening trade. There were fewer cars on the road, and fewer people on the esplanade. It was as if a truce had suddenly been agreed, and the Saint welcomed the lull.

It was cooler now, and the leaves of the palm trees along the Boulevard rustled in a freshening breeze. Simon breathed deeply as he walked, to clear his mind and cleanse his body.

He turned in at the driveway entrance of the private marina and began to stroll along its quais, choosing a course that showed no conspicuous purpose but which could not fail to bring him eventually in sight of the *Protégé,* wherever it was berthed. As, much sooner than later, it did.

For a cabin cruiser, *Protégé* looked even more opulent at close range than when he had just spotted it that afternoon. Five noughts' worth of powered luxury were calculated to gladden the heart of any man whose knowledge of the sea and ships extended past the municipal boating lake. Simon stood on the far side of the wharf behind a stack of barrels, ready to duck out of sight if Demmell appeared, but the only activity came from a crewman leaning over the stern rail and sending a grey pall of smoke into the air from an ancient pipe.

He was about to retrace his steps when he saw the black Renault turn through the parking lot. He sank down behind the nearest cover as it cruised up to the stern of the *Protégé*.

Cartwright was sitting in the back, apparently engaged in a heated argument with his driver. A map was produced, and although the conversation was inaudible the gestures of the two men plainly pantomimed their disagreement. The *Protégé*'s crewman watched the scene with a half smile, and when the driver wound down the window and in pidgin French asked for his advice he was happy to leave the boat and walk over.

It was one of the slickest models of kidnapping that the Saint had ever had the pleasure of watching, and it appealed to the artist in his soul.

The crewman walked to the car, and as he approached, the driver got out and spread the map on top of the trunk. The sailor bent over to consider it and Cartwright simply opened his door and hoisted the startled man backwards into the car. The driver jumped back in and was slewing the car around even before the rear door was closed. Simon saw Cartwright's arm rise and fall once, and the sailor gave no further sign of resistance.

The Saint waited until the car had disappeared before rising from his hiding place and turning back from the port, his brain vibrating with questions for which he could find no ready answers.

Cartwright's interest in Demmell he could understand, but what was Demmell's interest in Maclett? And why hijack a sailor? Why not take Demmell? Simon again ran over the conversations he had had with Maclett and Curdon, and an idea began to form in his mind. He rejected it at first, but it refused to be dismissed, and the more it was considered the more plausible it became.

He arrived back at the Bellevue without any clear-cut solutions but was the proud possessor of a theory supported more by intuition than by evidence and he had the absolutely firm conviction that there would be more fun and games before the night was over.

6

Gaby swung his car through the obligatory one-way detours to the main road that climbs towards Mougins. Samantha turned to the Saint.

"Where are we going?"

"To the best of the new restaurants on this coast, where they say you can gorge like a discriminating glutton without getting fat. I hope your appetite is up to the challenge."

"I hope my figure can stand it."

Again Simon detected the trace of an accent. Scandinavian perhaps, he reflected; that would certainly go with the hair and the eyes.

They had only made the smallest of small talk since leaving the hotel, while each discreetly studied the other. Simon frequently caught her sidelong glances, noticing that behind the ready smile her eyes were suspicious. Her lack of conversation came not from shyness or reserve but was the caution of a businessman intent on not revealing anything which might help a rival.

She had appeared in the lobby precisely at the appointed hour. Such punctuality had not surprised him, somehow it was in keeping with the vibrations he had registered. She had exchanged the sheer white dress of the afternoon for a flowing lemon silk evening gown that swept about her as she moved, reminding him of an exotic butterfly. Her only jewellery was a thin gold chain that hung around a neck which needed no other adornment to underline its grace, and a solitaire diamond ring on her right hand. A more subtle fragrance had replaced the perfume that had invaded his return to consciousness a few hours before.

The car stopped outside a refurbished old stone building a little below the road on one slope of a small ravine which had been worn geological eons ago by the millstream from which the building had originally been designed to profit. Inside, the decor and furnishings were luxurious in a Provençal-antique style and a world away from the functional modernism of equivalent restaurants in Cannes.

They were conducted to a table set for two by an open window overlooking a small lawn and the reed-grown valley.

"An apéritif?" Simon asked, echoing the maître d'hôtel's automatic question. "Or are you a straight champagne addict?"

"As a compromise, I'll have a champagne cocktail."

"For me, a vodka martini–shaken, stirred, on the rocks, and with a twist of lemon."

The Saint had chosen the Vieux Moulin with care. It was a favourite retreat of his when the constant movement of Cannes began to irritate. It had the advantage of allowing two people to talk without sharing their conversation with hovering waiters and too proximate fellow-diners. The food was sublime and the setting was deliberately, almost overtly, romantic. Modesty had never been one of the Saint's failings and he knew to the finest part of a degree the effect his personality could have on even the hardest of feminine hearts, especially when aided by fine food and wine and artistic lighting.

Samantha nibbled at an olive.

"For a scientist, you certainly have style."

"Well, I used to be a marine biologist, but I got in trouble for eating the specimens. Especially the caviar."

Samantha giggled.

"I don't believe you're a scientist at all."

Simon was saved from finding an instant reply by the arrival of their drinks. When he had ordered their meal, he asked: "What do you do for your yacht and your suite at the hotel and that rock on your finger?"

"I peddle genius."

"You what?"

Samantha lowered her empty glass and casually reached across and appropriated Simon's.

"I run an employment agency called Genius Inc. We don't handle anyone with an IQ of less than 150."

Simon retrieved his half-empty glass and placed it well out of her reach.

"But surely geniuses don't need people to find them jobs?"

"You'd be surprised how stupid really brilliant people can be. They're usually working for about a third of what they're really worth. We help them to get their market value."

The waiter brought the artichokes barigoule, a speciality of the house, and they waited while he served it. Samantha reached over and gouged out a sample from the Saint's plate. Simon watched in amused disbelief as she ate it and then proceeded to attack her own.

"How was it?"

"Delicious."

"How's yours?" Simon's fork sped towards her plate but she parried it with the adroitness of a fencing master.

"About the same."

"Is that why you're here, prospecting for genius?"

"We go to all the scientific congresses, that's the kind of talent that pays off today."

Samantha's hand absentmindedly moved towards the Saint's wineglass, but he managed to capture it in time.

"It certainly seems to have paid off for you."

"I was in a hurry. I was hungry until I was fifteen. Now I play to win."

"You certainly play hard. When do you get your black belt?"

Samantha started, and for a moment Simon thought he was going to face a blank denial, but she only lowered her head in mock shame.

"So you guessed."

"It wasn't exactly the greatest piece of detection work since Sherlock Holmes. And Demmell—who, or rather what, is he?"

"Demmell is a fool, but a useful one. He works for me, mainly I think because he knows I'm not attracted to him and he's continually trying to prove himself. Male ego and all that. All the same, I couldn't have you beating him up. One has a duty to one's employees, you know."

"Of course, everyone knows that."

If Samantha caught the Saint's sarcasm she showed no signs of being offended by it.

"Was it your idea that he should tear my room apart?" he enquired casually.

"Oh no, never. I'm afraid he's rather impetuous."

Somehow the conversation was not running along the lines he had sketched out for it, and he found her mixture of businesslike frankness and wide-eyed innocence rather hard to take. Simon leaned across and took her hand in his.

"Would you like to marry me?"

Samantha helped herself to some more of the Saint's artichoke and smiled.

"I can't wait. But we'll have to work out how I can divorce two husbands without convicting myself of bigamy."

The Saint toyed with the idea of proposing an ingenious double murder, but realized that this line of badinage was getting nowhere. He decided that since she must have had her own motives for accepting his invitation, he might as well play along until she was forced to take the initiative.

But in spite of his restraint, the conversation remained on a plane of sophisticated triviality, until the meal was finished and the head waiter was routinely proposing coffee and liqueurs.

"Why don't we go back to my suite at the hotel?" Samantha said. "It's got a balcony with a better view than this."

"I'd love to see it," said the Saint, and asked for his bill.

The man was concerned, he was unaccustomed to guests who ate each other's food, drank from each other's glass, and then left in a hurry.

"Is everything all right, monsieur?"

Simon stood, and Samantha remained seated only long enough to finish the last of the wine.

"Everything is just fine," he replied, peeling the requisite notes from his roll and adding a large tip. "It's just that my wife worries if I'm late for dinner."

The maître d'hôtel smiled uncertainly, and was still trying to decipher the Saint's meaning long after he and Samantha had left the room, finally consoling himself with the thought that, as everyone knew, all foreigners were insane.

Gaby also was somewhat surprised to see them emerge so soon, but unlike the waiter, he didn't look for reasons. Simon glanced at his watch as he followed Samantha into the back of the car. Only about two and a half hours had elapsed since they had left the hotel, which was not long for a dinner engagement in the circumstances. But the Saint's intuition told him that the final good nights were not racing up on him.

Samantha nestled close, her head resting on his shoulder, and they spoke sparingly as Gaby obeyed his instructions and sent the Buick speeding back to Cannes.

Samantha's suite occupied a corner of the floor, providing a panorama of the bay town from the floodlit prison of the Man in the Iron Mask on the island of Ste. Marguérite on the left to the Suquet in the western background. She made no move to call for room service. Her arms hung loosely around the Saint's shoulders, and he could feel the warmth of her breath on his cheek.

Her voice barely rose above a whisper.

"If you're Sebastian Tombs of the blackboards and cobwebby laboratories, I'm Florence Nightingale."

Simon's lips brushed hers in a fleeting kiss.

"You minister most ably, Miss Nightingale."

Samantha drew back slightly, looking directly into his eyes. "Who are you really?"

"My name is Simon Templar."

The revelation of his true identity had, in the past, been known to provoke a number of reactions—fear, anger, and disbelief being the usual ones. But rarely had he experienced the response that Samantha displayed. She laughed.

"Simon . . . The Saint! Thank God, I thought you might be the Law. But you are working for Maclett?"

"Yes."

Samantha stopped laughing and looked thoughtful, moving away slightly.

"We must get together."

Simon's arms encircled her waist.

"I'm all for togetherness."

She ignored that interpretation for the moment.

"Help me persuade him to go and work in Moscow, and I'll split my fee with you." Samantha removed herself from his embrace and sat on the arm of a sofa.

"You sell people to the Communists?"

Samantha lit a cigaret and considered the glowing end pensively.

"Only a few of the best. Listen, it's not such a bad deal. The equivalent of two hundred thousand dollars a year, the big flat in Moscow, the dacha in the country, the box at the Bolshoi, and the big car, with no traffic jams because nobody else has one."

The Saint laughed.

"Sam, I'm afraid you're a cynic."

"That's just a name romantics call realists." She walked

slowly back to him, her arms sliding up the front of his jacket and resting on his shoulders. "Let's talk it over."

Her lips moved to meet his, stopping a fraction of an inch away.

"Keep talking," Simon murmured. "I don't make up my mind in a hurry."

In the event, the ensuing conversation was less than verbose, but it still gave the Saint no indication of what else Samantha had hoped to gain from it. Or if, indeed, there was anything . . .

He was sleeping peacefully in his own room when he was awakened by an insistent knocking on the door. As he rolled out of bed, a glance at his wrist watch showed him that it was nine in the morning–a not unreasonable hour for visitation, except that he was not expecting one.

The visitor was Emma, and she confronted him furiously.

"Where were you all night? I kept calling you."

"I was a bit late getting in. I had to go to an Arab chum's bar mitzvah."

She stormed in as he stood hospitably aside.

"What's going on? My father got a message to meet you at the port at half-past nine–"

"Which port?"

"I don't know, but it said opposite the Hôtel Méditerranée. I found the note in his room, so I thought I'd find out if you'd already left. Why–"

The Saint reversed his welcome abruptly, turning his back towards the door.

"I'm leaving now, as soon as I can get dressed. I'm afraid I overslept. Sorry, I just haven't time to explain. I'll see you later."

He physically pushed her out, unceremoniously but necessarily. As he ran an electric razor over his chin, splashed cold water on his face, and threw on the nearest shirt and slacks, he was cursing himself more than Samantha.

"Very neat." His thoughts were racing. "You keep me occupied while your people organize a snatch."

In front of the hotel, he looked around desperately for a taxi, for in such a locality, at that hour, the world was barely coming to life. But as if in answer to his prayer, a white Buick seemed to materialise.

"Le quai St. Pierre—et gazez!"

Gaby nodded, wrenching the wheel almost full circle and sending them squealing out of the hotel grounds. Ignoring the protesting horns and flashing lights of the cars that tried to block his way, he sped the taxi along the Boulevard.

Professor Maclett had, probably, chosen to make the rendezvous as a morning stroll along the sea front. Even now, it was not absolutely impossible for the Saint to keep his mythical appointment close to time. The early traffic on the Croisette was scanty, and in only a minimum of minutes Gaby was pulling into the parking lot beside the quay opposite the hotel.

The Saint was out of the car before it had stopped, his eyes frantically scanning the peaceful morning scene as he hurried along the wharf. Then, through a gap in the sardine-packed rows of boats, he saw an open launch creaming its way towards the open sea, and even from that distance he could identify the burly figure and flaming hair of Professor Maclett standing in the stern.

Gaby had climbed out of his cab and come up beside the Saint, following the line of his eyes. Simon turned to him.

"I need a boat. A fast boat."

Gaby pointed towards a speedboat berthed a little farther along the jetty. It was typical of the craft that earned a living for their owners by towing water skiers around the bay. A man was kneeling in the bow adjusting a mooring rope.

Gaby called to him: "Bonjour, Albert!"

The man turned, recognised him, and came aft to climb up onto the jetty.

"I want to hire your boat," said the Saint.

"At what time, m'sieu? I have a client at eleven."

"Now!"

Simon thrust a roll of hundred-franc notes into the man's hand, and had jumped down onto the boat and cast off while the startled owner was still counting them. He gunned the powerful engine into life and sent the boat purring out into the channel.

7

To avoid attracting the unwelcome attention of the maritime police, he had to make his way through the harbour at a speed that any Olympic swimmer could have surpassed without any exertion, and by the time he cleared the breakwater the launch he was following had taken a formidable lead.

As soon as he reached open water and was able to give the motor its head, the power of the propeller's churning blades lifted the bow of the light fibre-glass hull clear of the water. He stood with his legs slightly bent to absorb the shock of the continual pounding as the keel jounced over innocent wavelets that seemed to turn into ridges of solid wood. His hands caressed the wheel as he automatically followed the creaming wake of the launch.

His borrowed speedboat was nimble and fast, but the launch he was trailing was no lumbering tugboat either. After a few minutes, he could estimate that he could be sure of overtaking it, but that it would be anything but a short, swift chase.

He was still trying to figure out the wherefores of the operation. Was Maclett actually being kidnapped at gunpoint? Or had he been told that he was only being ferried to a more secret meeting place?

The launch was headed east-southeast towards the two islands that lie in parallel off the point of the small peninsula where the Croisette ends, on a course that would take it through the channel between Ste. Marguérite and Ste. Honorat. It would certainly get there before he could catch it.

They were not the only vessels headed in that direction. Already a few much larger yachts were cruising towards the same channel, both from the old port and the Port Canto, under orders to take up the best anchorages while their owners and passengers breakfasted, for it was a favourite spot for the luxuriously seaborne community to spend the day, sunning and swimming well removed from the less favoured crowds on the beaches. For many of those millionaire cruisers, it was the longest voyage they ever took.

Simon judged speed and distance with the expert eye of a professional sailor. When he overhauled the launch it would be well into the channel, among several other statelier craft jockeying for position in addition to the boats already berthed there. Whatever were the intentions of the people on the launch, the Saint did not want to make his pursuit too obvious.

The Saint was uncomfortably aware that if his pursuit became unmistakable and he then had the temerity to try to head off the launch he would simply be run down, and drawing alongside was the easiest way he could imagine to collect a bullet.

The wind whipped the early warmth of the sun from his skin, pulling at his clothes and hair as the spray flung back by the bow stung his eyes. The Saint grinned at the sound of the hull smashing down on the water, at the protest of the wind in his ears, at the way the morning, so peaceful and tame just a few minutes before, had suddenly become wild and free, at the way the muscles of his arms reacted to hold the speedboat on course when it bucked like a skittish colt.

It was for such moments that the Saint lived. They were the reason for his existence, the antidote to the humdrum organised mundanity of modern life. It had often been suggested that the Saint was born out of his time, that he should have lived in the days when men carried swords at their sides, that he would have been better suited to captaining a privateer in search of galleons on the Spanish Main; that he had no place in the drab days of the twentieth century. But the Saint knew that it is not the time that matters but the people who live in it. He knew that those who spend their present plaintively recalling another's past are not really yearning for those adventures so much as protecting themselves from the challenges of their own day. His own steed was a fast car, his frigate a speeding motorboat, but his spirit was as free as that of any highwayman or privateer.

But with all that, his tactical instincts, as lively as those of any pirate, suggested a possibly profitable switch. The Saint made it without consciously examining his decision.

With a touch of the wheel, he sent the speedboat veering to port, out of its direct trail of the launch that carried Maclett.

The launch continued on its way into the channel between the islands, while the Saint's speedboat swept into a parallel course opposite Ste. Marguérite. In a moment they were cut off from sight of each other. But the Saint figured that he had enough speed in hand to reach the eastern end of the island well ahead of the launch, swing around it, and meet the launch in the channel from an unexpected and apparently accidental head-on direction. Whatever the purpose of the party in the launch might be, his interception of it should take them completely by surprise.

He scanned the speedboat's cockpit for anything that might prove useful once he made the encounter. His glance fell on a metal box bolted to the side under the dashboard, and he leaned over and flicked it open, to find it contained a Very pistol and distress flares. Guiding the boat with only an occasional touch, he carefully fitted a cartridge and placed the pistol on the ledge behind the windshield.

Up to a point, his plan worked out exactly as he had envisioned it. He kept the speedboat headed towards Cap d'Antibes until well past the end of Ste. Marguérite, to stay safely away from the irregular reef which projects eastwards under water from the island, before making his U-turn back into the channel where the big yachts were parking for the day. And almost at once he saw the launch that he had previously been following, rushing towards him and away from the assemblage of statelier pleasure barges in the most sheltered center of the notch.

Simon cut his engine to a mere tick-over, and as the speedboat slumped in the water he slewed it directly across the path of the launch. He stood up in the cockpit, waving his arms in an unmistakeable request for communication.

Without slackening speed by a knot, the launch veered to miss him, but so closely that its water almost capsized the speedboat, and only the Saint's fantastic reflexes and co-ordinating muscles saved him from being thrown down into or bodily out of the bucking cockpit.

As he recovered some semblance of vertical balance, he saw that the launch was resuming its course, unchecked, and with the clearest intention of declining to be detained. Three silhouettes against the now glaring sunlight looked back, it seemed with callous derision.

The Saint seldom lost his temper, but something about that exercise in nautical boorishness got under his skin. With something akin to the conditioned response of a Western gunfighter, he snatched up the Very pistol from the ledge in front of him and fired. The flare sped across the water like a coloured comet and exploded as it landed in the open stern of the launch.

Billows of smoke engulfed the launch, and with great satisfaction he heard the engine splutter and die. He loaded another cartridge into the pistol and held it at the ready as he brought the speedboat alongside.

As he did so he realised he had been fooled, beautifully lured and brilliantly snared.

There were three men in the launch. They wore the rough denims of fishermen, and their language was as colourful as the flare that one of them was busy stamping out. But Professor Maclett was definitely not one of them.

The Saint did not stop to join an altercation but simply gunned the speedboat around and headed back out of the channel.

It had been a very slick operation, and he had outsmarted himself with his own clever maneuver to help it to succeed. While out of his sight behind the island, the launch had simply drawn alongside one of the big yachts anchored there and stopped to allow one of the fishermen he had seen to replace Maclett. Which testified to an impressive degree of organisation.

He would have dearly loved to have cruised on through the channel in the hope of identifying the boat that now had Maclett aboard, but he could not have done that without blatantly exposing himself. But as he circled back towards Cannes, his mind was racing back to the ridiculous theory that had been hatched during his return from the Port Canto that afternoon, which began to seem a great deal more sane and logical.

He nudged the speedboat alongside the wharf from which he had taken it, and had scarcely picked up the mooring when he became aware of a reception committee on the quayside.

A small dapper figure stepped forward.

"Monsieur Templar, I am Inspector Lebeau. You are under arrest for the kidnapping of Professor Andrew Maclett."

8

It was a little different from what the Saint had expected, but he accompanied Lebeau to the waiting car and allowed himself to be driven to the police station without protest.

He demanded a lawyer, and was told that he would have that privilege at the proper time. He asked for a consul to be contacted, and was assured that every formality would be observed. A request or permission to collect some things from his hotel was politely refused.

He could imagine how hot the telephone lines would soon become as the news of his arrest reached Paris and then London in time for the first editions of the evening papers. "SAINT ARRESTED!" He could almost see the headlines.

Lebeau was obviously pleased with his catch, for he personally conducted the Saint to his cell, even apologising for the quality of the accommodation and expressing a hypocritical hope that the unfortunate situation would soon be sorted out and all the truths established.

In France, under the still sacred Code Napoléon, a man is guilty until proven innocent, and therefore there is no reason why the amenities supplied while he awaits confirmation of that assumption should be anything above the minimum as far as comfort is concerned. The cells of the average city police station in Britain would rate as starred hotels compared with their counterparts across the Channel.

The Saint found himself in a room barely ten feet square, with rough concrete walls and a flagstone floor. Air came via a small barred window set high up in the wall opposite the door, and light from an unshaded bulb which, despite the smallness of the room, still managed to leave the corners in shadow. Two bunks hung couchettelike from one wall. A plain deal table and a couple of chairs, and a slop pail, were the only other furnishings.

Both bunks were occupied, and a third inmate sat huddled in a corner, head on knees and snoring loudly. The cuts and bruises on the faces of all three, and the stale smell of cheap wine, were silent evidence of the reasons for their presence.

Simon settled himself in the corner opposite the snorer. He took off his jacket and folded it to make a headrest. He had never before tasted the official hospitality of the Republic, but he possessed an almost mystical ability to relax completely in any situation where sound and fury would achieve nothing, conserving his energy for the moment when it could be exploded with the maximum effect.

The grating of a key in the lock interrupted his inventing of transcendental meditation, and he stood up and stretched his limbs hopefully. The visit, however, was not for him: the *agent* who came in ungently roused his cellmates and herded them into the corridor outside, where two more officers waited.

Simon watched as they were marched away, and protested: "If this is lunchtime, why am I left out?"

The warder, who had cautiously kept a safe distance from the Saint, replied with ponderous joviality: "This is not the Hôtel Negresco, but I will ask the room service waiter not to forget you."

The door slammed, and another half hour passed before it was opened again.

It was the same agent, with the same sense of humour.

"If you have a moment, the management would like a word with you."

"I have been saving a word for them," said the Saint pleasantly. "But I shall not sully your delicate ears with it."

With the reinforcement of two more agents, the Saint was delivered to Lebeau's office.

Sir William Curdon sat on Lebeau's right. He glared as Simon entered and coolly seated himself in the vacant chair opposite the inspector.

Lebeau smiled.

"Good morning again, Monsieur Templar, I hope you have found our facilities comfortable."

"Fabulous," said the Saint. "I shall be writing about them to the *Guide Michelin.*"

Curdon's fist thudded against the desktop and his voice shook.

"Damn this nonsense! Where is Maclett, Templar? What was that little boat ride all about?"

"Well, Willie, the fact is that swimming often damages the clothing, so I thought perhaps using a boat might—"

Lebeau cut him short.

"Your personal differences aside, Monsieur Templar, you were in the suspected vicinity. You arrived back, Professor Maclett did not."

The Saint shrugged.

"Inspector, I deeply regret arriving back."

"Lebeau, I want this man safe and sound in a jail cell until he tells us where he's got Maclett stashed!"

Curdon seemed about to turn into a cloud of steam, and Lebeau turned to the Saint with an apologetic gesture.

"I regret, but I am obliged to feel in favour of British intelligence."

"And I regret," said the Saint honestly, "that I haven't the faintest idea where Professor Maclett is now. Why doesn't British Intelligence know?"

"Lock him up again!" Curdon bellowed. "We'll get the truth out of him soon enough, however we have to do it. Let's talk again privately, Lebeau."

At a sign from Lebeau, the two escorting agents stepped forward, and the Saint stood up.

"I must let you into a state secret, Inspector," he said. "Where British Intelligence ought to be, there is apparently a boiled potato."

He tapped his head. Lebeau stared at him stonily. Simon smiled into Curdon's face.

"See you later, Willie."

The policeman held the Saint's arms as they walked back down the stairs towards the cells. The Saint offered no resistance until they reached the ground floor and were nearing the junction of two corridors. Ahead of them, a window ran from the floor almost to the ceiling. He had had a good look at it on his way up to the interview with Curdon and Lebeau and knew exactly what he had to do.

The Saint started to run, his arms closing around the waist of his escort and forcing them to do the same. Taken off their guard, the men had no alternative but to comply. The Saint charged towards the window with the force of a wounded bull, throwing himself forward at the last moment and shaking off their grip. Arms crossed over his face, shoulder turned to take the brunt of the impact, he launched himself at the glass.

The window dissolved into a thousand tiny knives that could have torn him to shreds, but he had learned in a hard school that the trick of passing through windows in that unorthodox fashion was to hit them with exactly the speed that would deflect the fragments before they could claw at the passing body.

He landed unscathed on the gravel-coated car park in a rolling somersault, his knees pulled high into his chest, arms still shielding his face and head. The sharp stones bit through the thin cotton of his shirt, grazing the skin beneath, but the Saint had no time to worry about a few trivial abrasions. He scarcely felt them, in the surge of excitement that came with his return to freedom.

He rolled over once before springing upright and racing towards the line of cars parked on the far side of the courtyard. A prowl car was backing into the centre of the quadrangle, and the Saint sprinted to head it off. Behind him, he could hear a chorus of confused shouts merging into the pounding of running feet. A flung baton hit him behind the knees and almost felled him, but the Saint split his stride like a hurdler and increased his speed.

The police car braked as its occupants, a plainclothes detective and his uniformed driver, became aware of the commotion. The offside door was flung open and the detective jumped out, running around the car towards the Saint, his hand grabbing for the holster inside his jacket. Simon jumped high, straightening in the air, his body becoming as rigid as an arrow. His heels landed squarely in the center of the man's chest, hurling him off his feet. The detective's mouth opened, but no sound emerged. With an expression of surprise still frozen on his face, he pitched backwards and lay still.

The Saint landed a yard from the car. The driver was half-way out of the door, a revolver in his hand. The Saint sprang forward, throwing every ounce of his weight against the door. The driver screamed as the metal sliced into him: his arm jerked upwards, and his gun barked harmlessly at the sky. Simon grasped his wrist and smashed his hand against the car, sending the revolver clattering away across the roof.

Still keeping his hold, the Saint stepped back, taking the driver with him, as his fist whipped around in a right cross to the chin. The man crumpled, and Simon slid in behind the wheel, flicking the gears into reverse and stamping on the accelerator to send the car bucking backwards. Then he skidded the car around and out of the quadrangle.

The scream of the engine drowned the sound of a shot, and the glass of the rear window seemed to shiver for an instant before exploding. Simon kept his foot pressed to the floor, holding the car on course as if such interventions were merely to be expected.

A pair of heavy wrought-iron gates hung at the arched entrance. Two guards were valiantly trying to pull them together, and they were already partly closed when the Saint reached them. He snaked between them, scraping one as he heeled over in a two-wheeled skid onto the road outside.

9

One hand searched the switches on the dashboard until he found the one which controlled the siren, and its insistent two-toned hooting split the air. The whole operation, from the time he had charged for the window to the moment he hit the road, had taken less than a minute but already another police car was swinging out of the station less than a hundred yards behind, and in the rear-view mirror he saw it overtaken by a powerful motorcycle that slipped through the traffic on the wrong side of the road.

Simon switched on the radio and listened to the unemotional voice of the central despatcher relaying the news of his escape and ordering road blocks to be set up on the major routes out of town. But the Saint had already decided that his best chance lay in drawing the chase through the narrow back streets until he could shake it off.

The traffic ahead stopped or swung to the side as soon as the drivers caught sight of the flashing lights or heard the blaring sirens, and the Saint zigzagged through them.

He threw the car around another corner of the maze, heading roughly towards the sea. His siren claiming priority over any law of the road, he threatened coronaries to oncoming drivers and forced those on his own side into the kerb.

A lorry attempted to dispute his right of way at a crossing and he skimmed the Citroën under its nose with inches to spare. The driver swung frantically away from the maniac who seemed to be doomed to extinction under his wheels and crashed into another van parked on the corner. As he made the next turn, Simon saw that the log jam he had left behind would effectively halt the police posse for several minutes, except perhaps for the motorcycle cop.

Now to make his passage less conspicuous, he switched off the siren as he came to the food market. A man pushed a barrow out from between two parked trucks and there was neither time nor room to avoid him.

The car ploughed into the side of the cart, tossing it into the air. Simon saw the bonnet buckle on impact and heard the crash of glass and rending metal. He swerved the car steeply to one side, just grazing a lamppost, and for twenty yards actually drove along the sidewalk before regaining the road. The front wheels should have been ripped from the axle, the twisted metal should have pushed the radiator and fan back into the engine block, the steering should have been shot to hell, but somehow the car kept on going.

The Saint looked in the mirror again and thought he saw the motorcycle far behind, momentarily blocked by the new obstacle, but unlike a car, it would not be detained for long.

As he came to a wider road nearer the Boulevard Jean Hibert, his eyes were searching for a possible hiding place. The entrance to the underground garage of a new apartment building caught them, and he wrenched the wheel to catapult the car into the opening. The move was so fast that he could dare to hope that he had finally eluded his pursuers, as he threw the car down the ramp into the dimly lit basement below.

He berthed the battered car in the handiest vacant space, and carefully started back towards the entrance on foot, edging his way between the rows of parked vehicles.

He had almost reached the ramp when the roar of a motorbike told him that his optimism had been premature and sent him ducking behind the nearest car.

The rider zoomed around the crypt and braked as soon as he saw the prowl car. He jerked the heavy bike onto its stand, and unclipped the holster at his side. Holding the pistol in front of him, he cautiously approached the car, his eyes sweeping from side to side as he walked. But the Saint was already behind him.

Simon closed in with two long strides that took him to within six inches of the man's back. He leaned forward and spoke softly in his ear.

"Avez-vous la plume de ma tante?"

The cop started to turn, but the Saint's fingers closed around his neck, digging into the somniferic pressure points on each side. The other's elbow rammed at Simon's stomach, but the Saint held his grip and the struggle was over in seconds. Simon dragged him behind the prowl car and removed his uniform jacket with the dexterity of a professional quick-change artist.

He bundled the unconscious man into the back of the car and pulled on the coat. Fortunately the *motard* was built on the lines of a healthy barrel, and what the jacket lacked in length, for the Saint's long, lean frame, it could make up from excess circumference. The eventual compromise was not too grotesque.

He did not bother with the boots and uniform breeches, which would almost certainly have been less adaptable anyhow. He had to trust that the light blue slacks he was already wearing would blend in well enough to get past any but the most hypercritical eye. The standard crash helmet and its visor covered enough of his face, and with that in place he mounted the motorcycle and rode up the ramp out of the garage.

He headed directly for the Croisette and back towards the Hôtel Bellevue, confident that that was the last place where the frantic search parties would be looking for him. The situation offered endless opportunities for sport, and he had to fight back the temptation to indulge them, contenting himself with snapping a smart salute to a senior officer addressing a squad of men opposite the Palais des Festivals as he rode past.

At the hotel, an assistant manager hurried over as he approached the concierge's desk.

"What are you doing here? The inspector said he would give strict instructions to his men to use the staff entrance."

Simon raised the visor of his crash helmet slightly, which allowed his hand to partly cover his face.

"I was sent to collect some things from Templar's room. I need the key."

"The inspector took it."

"Well, he never gave it to me. You'd better let me have a master key."

The man dithered, seemed about to quote the rules, and then noticed the looks his guests were giving the Saint. He gave a sign to the concierge, who produced a key with a massive brass tag and put it on the counter.

"And remember to leave by the staff entrance. We do not want the police in the public rooms."

The Saint shrugged.

"If you don't want us here, you shouldn't have people like Templar here either."

He turned away towards the elevators, aware that the eyes of everyone in the lobby followed him and breathed a long sigh of relief when the doors closed behind him.

There was no guard on the door to his room, and no one in the corridor to see him enter it. He peeled off the uniform jacket while he turned on the shower in the bathroom. All things considered it had not been the most satisfactory twenty-four hours of his life, he reflected as he impudently indulged in the luxury of the water.

His mind roamed back over the events of the previous night: the startled look on Samantha's face when Emma had announced her father's disappearance, the slickness of the decoy operation and the fact that the police were waiting for him when he returned empty-handed, the look in Curdon's eyes during their talk at the police station. The wild theory that had nagged him the night before no longer seemed insane; but there was still one angle that had to be tried, and the Saint realised just how little time he had in which to test it.

The shower washed away the aches of his body as well as the staleness of the police station cell, and the crispness of a complete change to fresh clothes seemed to pump fresh vitality into his body.

The room showed signs of having been subjected to a thorough search, but only his passport and personal papers had been removed. The Saint slid his hand along the back of the drawer in the bedside table and carefully freed the knife that he had left taped there.

He smiled as he strapped the supple leather sheath to his left forearm. Simon Templar disliked guns in principle, considering them crude and noisy. It is relatively easy to kill a man when you cannot see his eyes, almost as simple as sitting behind a desk and ordering the murder of thousands. It is more difficult to throw a knife with the speed and sureness of a bullet, or to use it when so close that you can hear the beat of the other man's heart. The Saint could perform tricks with that slender blade that would make a circus knife thrower blanch. They had been together for a long time, and in times of peril the Saint felt naked without the reassuring pressure of the leather nestling against his skin.

He took the assistant manager's advice and went down to the ground floor in the service elevator, slipping out of the hotel through a side door and cautiously making his way around to the car park.

Gaby's taxi stood at the end of the rank, and Simon opened the rear door to slip in, crouching low between the seats.

Gaby glanced up from his paper but did not look around, simply adjusting the mirror until the Saint came into focus.

He held the paper so that Simon could see it.

"I thought you were a guest of our celebrated Inspector Lebeau."

The Saint smiled and shook his head.

"I didn't like the accommodation, so I decided to leave."

Gaby laughed and switched on the engine.

"Where to?"

"The Port Canto. Quick as you can."

Already Gaby was heading his Buick towards the Boulevard.

"You are always in a hurry, *n'est-ce pas?*"

"Life is short, and I always have so much to do," Simon apologised.

He risked a quick look out of the side windows. There seemed to be police on every corner and he hurriedly sank down again out of sight, pulling a travelling rug over himself.

The taxi driver intrigued him. The man always seemed to be available, it was almost as if he lived in his cab.

"Tell me—don't you ever go home?"

"I have to make my living."

"I hope it will not be endangered because of me."

Gaby laughed again.

"For certain clients," he said, "it is a pleasure to bend the rules."

Gaby drove through the private parking entrance with a familiar wave to the guard, and followed the Saint's directions to the place where Samantha's cabin cruiser had been.

Simon studied the scene with dismay. The quay where *Protégé* had been berthed before was empty. If it was *Protégé* that the launch carrying Maclett had rendezvoused with between the islands, as the Saint had now concluded, the fast cruiser had not returned to port. Was it still out there? Or, much more likely, where was it speeding now?

The Saint swore, and Gaby turned his head.

"You want another boat?"

Simon grinned ruefully.

"Not unless it has wings."

Gaby thought for a moment.

"I don't know of any boats with wings, but I have a friend who has them. You would like to meet him?"

Mystified, the Saint could only say: "I'd be delighted."

Gaby explained as he turned the car and drove back along the Croisette.

"My friend is a helicopter pilot for the sea rescue service."

"Will he help us?" The Saint did not try to keep the excitement out of his voice.

"I do not know, but he owes me a favour, several of them."

Gaby followed the coast road from the old port towards La Napoule but turned off at La Bocca, taking the inland route towards Mandelieu, where the Saint remembered that there was a small airfield.

The Buick finally stopped at the edge of a concrete landing pad. Two bright red helicopters stood beside a couple of ramshackle huts. A man in flying gear approached, and threw his arms around the taxi driver as if he were greeting a long-lost brother.

Simon stayed in the car while Gaby explained their problem. After a conversation that appeared to consist more of arm-waving gestures than words, Gaby called him over.

"He will help you, but only if you promise to say that you forced him at the point of a gun to take you, if anything goes wrong."

The Saint promised, and was led to the nearest helicopter. Gaby climbed in after him, saying: "I have come so far, and I have always wanted to ride in one of these."

The blades whirred into life and they lifted clear of the pad. The Saint navigated, searching the sea below.

On the face of it, it might have seemed like a real wild-goose chase, but he was gambling on a hunch that after all those elaborate preparations the *Protégé* would not just be moving along to the next nearest marina. Much more likely was yet another rendezvous southward, beyond sight of land, and out there in the open sea there were not so many cabin cruisers travelling that it would be hard to spot one from the air.

After what seemed an eternity he recognized a white hull racing southeast, towards Corsica, and under his direction the pilot banked his craft on a course that would bring them over her stern.

Despite the cruiser's power, there was no chance of her outrunning the copter, and the pilot easily countered her turns to stay a steady fifty feet above her.

Samantha was at the wheel, with Demmell beside her. Simon told the pilot to go lower, and quickly broke out the rescue harness.

"I'm going down," he said. "Tell Gaby how to work this gear."

They were still fifteen feet above the pitching cruiser when the Saint slid out of the cabin and began to be winched down. As he did so, Demmell ran down into the cabin under the bridge. As Simon prepared for the final descent, Demmell re-emerged with an automatic in his hand. He braced himself against a stanchion and took two-handed aim.

Without sparing the time to calculate the odds, the Saint let everything go and plummeted down towards him.

10

Demmell's finger jerked at the trigger. The bullet passed so close that Simon felt the wind of its passage fan his cheek. Frantically Demmell leapt aside, but the Saint twisted his body as he fell and cannoned into him. They crashed to the deck together.

Simon's breath was momentarily forced from his lungs as he landed on top of Demmell. Every bone jarred with the impact, pain shooting like lightning along his legs and back. Demmell lay still beneath him, spread-eagled against the planking, his eyes staring sightlessly at the sky. A thin trickle of blood was slowly creeping from the crown of his head, and only the slight heaving of his chest showed that he was still alive.

The Saint staggered to his feet. His legs felt like putty, and he held onto the side rail while he regained his wind and the mastery of his limbs.

Samantha still stood at the wheel, desperately trying to shake off the helicopter, but the pilot matched her move for move. Simon looked up into two eyes as cold and hard as his own.

"Stop the engines."

The girl ignored him, spinning the wheel and heeling the boat hard to starboard. The Saint felt the deck tilt and grabbed at the rail again to stop himself falling. He groped his way towards the sheer ladder that led from the deck where he was to the flying bridge and pulled himself up it.

Samantha looked around as he arrived beside her.

"You pig!"

He had hardly expected an effusive welcome, but the depth of hatred in her voice surprised him.

Nevertheless, he smiled tolerantly.

"I hope you'll excuse me dropping in like this."

He stepped towards the wheel as Samantha released her grip on it. She stood to one side as he cut the engines and the boat shuddered and lost way.

The Saint's attention was focussed on the helicopter as he signalled to the pilot that he was safe but to remain close, and it was only by chance that he caught the sudden movement to his right. He ducked and turned as a pair of powerful binoculars flashed past his head and hurtled overboard.

Samantha was wearing only shorts and a bikini top of minimal proportions, neither of which was in any way adequate to the task of concealing the perfection of her body, and Simon regretted that she seemed to be so out of tune with the ideas that such a costume would normally be calculated to inspire.

He straightened up, wagging a finger in solemn admonishment.

"Naughty, naughty."

The girl glared at him.

"I wish I'd killed you."

The Saint approached cautiously, a slight lingering soreness in his neck reminding him of her ability to fulfill her wish. But she did not make any of the countermoves that he was prepared for as he picked up a lifebelt that hung beside him and suddenly dropped it over her head, and forced it down over her shoulders to where the hole in it, conflicting with her exquisite chest measurement, was a perfect fit to pinion her arms to her sides as effectively as if they had been roped there.

"I think you could do with some time to reflect on your evil ways and the inhospitality you show to unexpected guests," he murmured, and swung himself nimbly down the ladder which he had scaled only a few moments before.

A stream of expletives culled from a dockside dictionary followed him, but the Saint didn't stay to appreciate the scope of her vocabulary.

Forward from the open after deck, immediately below the flying bridge, was the small but comfortable saloon-cum-charthouse, and at the other end of that a companionway led down to the forward quarters. Simon was halfway towards it when he heard the shot and the splintering of wood a couple of inches above his head.

He knew he could never reach the opening befor the gunman corrected his aim and nailed him, and he was stranded too far into the saloon to spring back out again to safety. The only alternatives were a second more accurate bullet or surrender. The Saint considered both in a fraction of a second, and raised his hands slowly so that his move was clearly visible to the man in the shade below.

The man came up the companionway warily, his gun aimed steadily at the Saint's stomach. Simon gradually lowered his arms until the palms of his hands rested on top of his head. The fingers of his right hand slid beneath his left cuff, feeling for the handle of his throwing knife.

There was the sound of a heavy bump overhead, which the Saint knew must be connected with Samantha's efforts to free herself, but it made the sailor look up in alarm. And in that instant of distraction the Saint's hand flashed forward, the knife flying through the air in a silver blur. The man screamed as the blade sliced across his knuckles and the pistol fell from his fingers.

Simon had started to follow the knife even before it had found its mark. The man was staring stupidly at his blood-covered hand and made no move to fight. Simon kicked the gun aside before unleashing a straight left that contained every gram of his strength to put the unfortunate sailor out of his misery.

He stepped over the body and retrieved his knife, fastidiously wiping it on the sailor's T-shirt before slipping it back into its sheath. Then he knelt down and inspected the man's wound. Satisfied that he was in no danger of bleeding to death, Simon left him and went down the companionway.

The steps led to a narrow passageway. The first door on one side opened onto a small cabin that was almost entirely taken up by two bunks and a couple of lockers. The bottom bunk was curtained off, and the Saint stood to one side and swished back the drapes. The crewman he had seen taken by Cartwright and his henchman the previous afternoon lay there in a drugged sleep.

Simon winced at the state of the man's face. It looked as if someone had used a razor to play noughts and crosses. Bandages were rolled around the top of his head, reaching down over the ears to meet similar repair work around his neck. One eye was hidden beneath a soft pad, while the other was bruised purple and so badly swollen that only a thin slit between the lids showed that there was still a pupil beneath.

The Saint drew the curtain and stepped back into the passage. The slight narrowing of his eyes was the only visible sign of the anger that burned within. He cursed himself for not having prevented Cartwright from taking the man, even though he realised that there was no way he could have guessed the agent's intention. The scarring of the sailor had been no haphazard affair but a methodically and expertly executed job of torture. He could only guess at the reason for it, but he longed for a chance to let Cartwright experience similar suffering.

Another door opened onto the galley, and there were two guest cabins which were slightly larger than those for the crew, as well as the predictable sanitary facilities. Simon searched every cupboard and even looked under the bunks, also into the tiny engine room and hold.

In the end, just one thing was certain: Professor Maclett was not on board.

"And then there were none," he reflected quietly as he returned to the saloon.

The crewman was just beginning to revive, and the Saint pulled him to his feet, half carrying, half dragging him below and locking him in the cabin with his injured colleague.

Samantha's struggles had succeeded in freeing one arm, with devastating consequences to her skimpy bikini top, when the Saint returned to the bridge. She glared at him implacably.

"Been having fun?"

"Where's Maclett?"

"How the hell should I know? You're Mr. Bright Guy, you tell me."

Simon grasped her roughly by the shoulders and shook her, his eyes drilling into hers.

"Stop playing the spoilt little girl. If you haven't got him, why are you running away?"

"I'm running away because I don't want to end up like Pierre."

"Pierre? The sailor with the facelift?"

"Yes. Curdon's bully-boy gave me two hours to leave Cannes or get the same treatment. No lousy professor is worth that kind of risk. When I saw the helicopter, I thought it was him coming after me just to make sure."

The final piece of the jigsaw locked into place. Simon felt the satisfying glow of knowing his theory had been correct, but it was cooled by the sickening realisation that he might be too late to do anything about it.

It had been a very simple ploy that had succeeded solely because it was so basic. He had been searching under stones when all the time the creature he hunted had been basking on top of the biggest rock of all, astute enough to understand that the Saint would overlook him just because he was not hiding. The trick with the fishing boat that morning had made him think of the sea and yachts, putting Samantha in the spotlight and the Saint in jail. And when that had failed, the enemy had sent Samantha packing, knowing that the Saint would try and stop her, all the while losing valuable time on a trail of irresistible red herrings.

"Our friend is quite a fisherman," Simon mused as he leaned out of the bridge and waved the hovering copter lower.

"Pardon?"

"Forget it, Sam."

Simon caught the swinging harness and hooked it on. "It's been nice seeing you, but I'm afraid I must fly. Perhaps we'll bump into each other again some time."

Demmell was beginning to revive and Samantha would soon have help with her Houdini efforts. But for several minutes yet she would be incapable of taking any offensive action against the Saint's departure. She looked up in raging impotence as he was winched aloft.

"If we do," she shouted, "I hope I'm driving a tank instead of a yacht!"

Simon laughed and waved a generous adieu. His last glimpse of her was as she turned back towards the semi-conscious Demmell with a withering contempt in her eyes and a stream of invective on her lips.

The pilot and Gaby looked questioningly at the Saint as he unbuckled himself in the cabin.

"A loud bark up a very wrong tree, I'm afraid." Simon pointed roughly northwards. "Home, James, and don't spare the horses."

As they flew he explained what had happened not so much to illuminate his companions as to sort out the details in his own mind. He studied the aerial maps and located Curdon's villa, pointing it out to the pilot.

"Can you take me there?"

The pilot nodded and banked the helicopter over Antibes, swinging slightly towards the east and flying high until they were directly over the villa.

Simon could make out two cars parked in the driveway, Cartwright's Renault and Curdon's silver-grey Mercedes. The swimming pool was empty and but for the presence of the cars the villa might have been deserted. Behind the house was a small area of lawn circled by a belt of trees, beyond them a barren stretch of hillside that could have been recently cleared for some new building.

"I want you to fly over the villa and then double back, come in below the tree line so that there is as little chance as possible that we will be spotted by anyone in the house."

The pilot did as he was instructed, flying over the brow of the hill and then skimming back barely ten feet from the ground to bring the helicopter to earth at the edge of the trees.

"I don't know how long I shall be," Simon said. "How long can you wait for me?"

The pilot shrugged.

"I'm not on duty until this evening, so you can have until then if you wish. Anyway, as far as I am concerned you have hijacked me and therefore how can I argue?"

Simon slapped him on the back.

"*Merci.* You are a true philosopher."

He climbed out of the craft but barred Gaby from following.

"I can't allow you to risk your neck, Gaby."

The taxi driver looked crestfallen. Simon punched him playfully on the shoulder.

"Don't worry, *mon vieux.* You may get more excitement than you can handle before long."

The man's face brightened.

"I hope so. It is dull for a driver to become only a passenger, you know."

Simon nodded.

"I understand."

He waved and was gone. He had an almost supernatural ability to arrive or depart as he wished, sometimes, without those around him being immediately aware of his coming or going.

He merged into the band of trees passing like a wraith between the trunks, his feet making no sound on the carpet of dry cones and pine needles.

He had forgotten more about field craft and the skill of stalking than most white men ever learn. He had been taught by those whose existence depended on their ability to master their environment and to control it with the aid of only the most primitive of weapons and the minimum of disturbance to the balance of life around them, whether that environment was the steaming jungles of Borneo and Brazil or the dry savannahs of Africa.

He reached the final line of trees and stood behind them, as still as any of their trunks. Only his eyes moved as he judged distances and angles of sight.

The rear of the villa seemed to consist mainly of windows, and with twenty yards of open ground separating the nearest tree from the house anyone who happened to look out of a window could not fail to see him. But there was one consolation: most of the windows on the ground floor were open, and if the alarm was not raised immediately when he left the protection of the trees, he would be able to get inside the house before anything could be done about it.

A pair of french windows opened onto a small patio, and the Saint raced towards them. He covered the distance with the long sure strides of the trained athlete, and stood for a moment outside, waiting for any shout or commotion that might warn that he had been seen. Hearing none, he stepped into the villa.

He found himself in a spacious dining room furnished with Empire chairs and sofas, oil paintings and gilt-framed mirrors, but he did not linger to admire the decor. He passed through it quickly into the corridor outside, which apparently bisected the villa, connecting the entrance hall in the center with the twin wings of the building.

Simon flitted along it, peering into every room. Most were shrouded in dust sheets, and only a couple of sitting rooms and a study looked as if they had been recently used. He reached the hall and was considering whether to go upstairs or continue the search at the other end of the ground floor when a door opened a few yards in front of him.

He stepped back into the shadow of the stairs as Cartwright emerged, carrying a tray full of bottles and glasses. He looked as scrubbed and immaculate as when the Saint had first met him, except for a long bruise that disfigured his cheek where the fire extinguisher had connected. The Saint resisted an almost overwhelming desire to get his fingers around that slender throat, but contented himself with watching Cartwright disappear into a room at the far end of the corridor.

He could hear Emma's voice clearly as the door was opened: "Daddy, I was afraid you'd been spirited off to the Russians or something."

Simon moved swiftly along the passage and stood close to the door. Maclett's rich Scottish accent was unmistakeable.

"As a matter of fact, I am. Y'know I've had t'claw 'n scratch m'way through, don't y'lass. All me life. Well, I've got t'be sure it comes to something."

"But what are you talking about? Sir William, what's going on?"

Curdon's tone was as smooth and polished as if he were addressing a committee of civil servants.

"Our Official Secrets Act says that what your father has to offer may not be offered. National security and all that. So he's chosen to go where he and his work will find proper appreciation."

"Emma, y'have t'understand." Maclett's gruff tones were soft, almost pleading. "The Russians've promised me m'work will be used t'benefit everyone. I've been planning t'go all along. I couldn't tell ye."

Emma sounded close to tears.

"But Sir William, you're D16. You represent our government!"

"After twenty years of loyal poverty, miss, I am now taking

the opportunity of representing me. And it is time to go, Professor."

"Daddy, no! Please!"

"I do love ye, lass. And I'll send fer ye once I've settled in."

"Daddy, for God's sake!"

"I pray you'll decide to come. Think on it, Emma. Y'know y're all I have in this world."

Simon decided that the touching scene should go unwitnessed no longer. He drew the throwing knife from its sheath, well aware of its inadequacy against the two guns he was almost certainly going to face. He opened the door and smiled into the four astonished faces that turned towards him.

"Hello, kiddies," he drawled. "Is this a private defection, or can anyone join in?"

11

Simon Templar savoured the surprise he had caused. He held the knife lightly between the tips of his thumb and forefinger, pointing it at the centre of the space between Curdon and Cartwright, ready to throw at the first of the two to make a move.

Emma was the first to recover from the shock of his sudden appearance.

"Simon! I thought you were . . ."

The Saint smiled, but his eyes never left the two men.

"Yes, so did Willie . . . stop that!"

Cartwright's hand had been sliding towards his jacket pocket. At the Saint's command he froze, but his fingers stayed poised above the flap.

"I can throw this before either of you can draw but you know I can only throw it once, so you'll just have to decide which one wants to be a dead hero."

Simon looked at Curdon, the sarcastic praise of his words soured by the contempt in his voice.

"A neat trick, Willie. You almost had me fooled, and you certainly put it over on the professor like a master."

Maclett stepped forward, and the Saint slid away from the door so that he could still keep the two agents in clear view.

"Listen, laddie, this is no concern of yours! I know ye have acted from t'best motives, but I told ye I don't need yer help. I'm not being forced. I'm going of me own free will."

"No, Professor, you only think you are. They've trapped you. If I wasn't here, try leaving this room and see just how much freedom you really have. They've got too much invested in you to allow you to change your mind."

The Saint's voice was utterly calm and reasonable, in spite of the almost melodramatic setting, trying to connect with the rational functions of a scientific brain.

"They've sold you as good a line of hokum as I've ever heard. Sure, they'll look after you in Moscow. You'll be the biggest propaganda weapon they've had in a decade. They'll pamper you with every comfort and provide every facility for your research work, and if that's all you really want then you'd better go."

He continued relentlessly: "But there's more, much more. You'll never be able to make a telephone call without knowing that someone is listening. You'll never be allowed to walk down the street without seeing someone following you. You'll never be allowed to leave the country, a country that's a world away from the one you know. You'll be betraying your country. That may not mean much at the moment, but it will later. The Russians don't respect a traitor any more than the countrymen he betrays. You're not even selling out for ideological reasons, but for money and prestige. They'll spit in your face and slap you on the back at the same time."

Maclett glowered at him with the resentment of a stubborn

bull. He was the living personification of the fact that genius can exist without a vestige of common sense.

"Why should I believe ye rather than them? It's no good trying to talk me out of it. Me mind's made up. Now stand aside. I'm going to walk out of that door, and neither you nor that toothpick is going to stop me."

Simon moved out of the professor's path.

"Go ahead, Professor. You too, Emma. But Willie and smiling boy are staying."

Curdon and Cartwright were standing a yard apart to the Saint's left, with Emma forming the third point of a triangle on his right. Maclett was standing in the open doorway behind Simon. Emma started towards her father, walking diagonally across the room. No one could have blamed her—she was unaccustomed to the intricacies of such situations, and the Saint recognised the danger too late.

Emma came between the Saint and Cartwright, giving Cartwright the second's chance he needed to reach the gun in his pocket. Cartwright gripped the girl around the waist, using her body as a shield, and the Saint found himself staring into the business end of a .38 without the faintest chance of escape or counter.

"Drop it, Templar."

Simon let his knife fall.

"Kick it towards me."

Again the Saint did as he was told. Cartwright released the girl, stooped, and picked up the knife. Curdon had also drawn his automatic, and the Saint raised his arms.

Emma ran to her father and buried her head in his shoulder. Maclett patted her hair as he would have a baby.

"Don't be afraid. He wouldn't have hurt you. He had to do it."

"Don't be so sure, Professor," said the Saint. "Our little lad likes hurting people—don't you, sonny?"

"Shut your mouth!"

Cartwright stepped menacingly towards the Saint, but Curdon intervened.

"All right, Cartwright, you can settle your personal score later."

He turned to Emma and the professor.

"Nothing has changed, Miss Maclett. I'm afraid you will have to stay here until your father is safely away. You can take a scheduled flight later and join him when the fuss has died down. Cartwright will look after you."

"You mean I'm a prisoner?"

"Of course not. But you must understand that we can hardly have you returning to town so soon, in case you let slip what has happened."

Maclett kissed his daughter on the forehead.

"Don't worry, lass, you'll come to no harm."

Curdon looked at his watch.

"Now, Professor, we really must be going."

Curdon made to lead the way, but Maclett stopped him.

"What about Templar?"

Sir William smiled reassuringly.

"Don't worry, he'll come to no harm. We are not gangsters, Professor. We leave that sort of thing to Mr. Templar. He'll be released with your daughter. I understand the police are rather anxious to talk to him."

The roar of the Mercedes engine faded into the distance. Emma sat staring at the floor without seeing the pattern of the carpet. Cartwright and the Saint faced each other across the centre of the room.

Simon studied the other man. Cartwright's gun hand was steady, but his other trembled slightly as he took a cigaret from the box on the table and lit it. He inhaled deeply. Simon was unsure whether it was an affected gesture or simply an act of habit finally opting in favour of Cartwright's need for a smokescreen. The exit of Curdon and the professor had created a vacuum, and the agent was uncertain how to fill it. A new tension began to edge the silence of the room.

The Saint knew that Emma's presence was the sole reason he was still alive. Curdon's promise concerning his safety had been a straight lie, and everyone but the professor had recognised it as such. He had as long to live as the time that needed to elapse before Emma could safely be taken back to town. To figure just how long that might be, he had to know Curdon's plans.

His gaze drifted over Cartwright's sartorial affectations with the same mocking insolence as he had given them at the hotel twenty-four hours before.

"The party's flat now that the grown-ups have left. What do we do next, junior? Play charades?"

Cartwright affected indifference to the Saint's taunt.

"Sit down, Templar."

He indicated the seat next to Emma. The Saint sat, and Cartwright backed to the window and looked out, careful to keep him covered all the time.

They sat in silence. Emma seemed sunk in shock. The Saint considered a score of ways in which the tables could be turned, and dismissed them one by one. Cartwright looked at his watch ten times in five minutes.

Suddenly the Saint guessed at the cause of his nervousness. From the moment he had entered the room he had felt that something, or someone, was missing from the scene.

"If you're waiting for that driver of yours," he said, "you're going to have a very long wait."

It was a random cast, but the way Cartwright started at his words told the Saint that it had hooked home.

"What do you mean?"

Simon began to reel in the line.

"Well, you don't suppose I walked in here alone armed only with a knife, do you?" The Saint's lazy drawl was condescending.

Cartwright, who had been perched on the window shelf, suddenly became aware of the target he offered to anyone in the grounds. He stood up and crossed over to the Saint.

"Explain."

Simon sighed as if summoning up the patience to spell out a simple fact to a backward child.

"I didn't come on this jaunt singlehanded. There are two of my pals outside."

Cartwright's eyes searched the Saint's face, trying to detect the lie but meeting only a smiling mask.

"I don't believe you. From what I've heard about you, it would be part of your style to charge in on your own."

"Then where is your driver?"

It was a good question and one to which the Saint would have liked an answer himself.

"You're bluffing."

Simon consulted his watch.

"I've been here for twenty-five minutes. I left instructions that if I wasn't back in half an hour they were to come and collect me. So you don't have long to wait to find out whether or not I'm bluffing."

Emma looked up as the Saint's words penetrated her despair, and Simon turned to her.

"Where was Curdon planning to take your father?"

"To the aero club. He has a private plane waiting to fly them to East Germany. They originally intended to rendezvous with a Russian freighter in the Med, but you stepped in and made that too dangerous."

Simon's mind ran over the route they would take. Driving fast, it would be a full half-hour's journey, and they already had a fifteen-minute lead. Every second lost now reduced his chances of catching them.

Cartwright was back at the window, peering out cautiously and using the curtains to screen his body. There was a fifteen-foot gap between him and the Saint and not a chance of covering half that distance without collecting a bullet.

Emma was looking at the Saint, her eyes holding his, imploring him to do something. Simon knew that with her help there was an outside chance. Had she been Samantha he would not have hesitated to take it, but there was a giant question mark over her probable reactions to the plan he was formulating. If it went wrong, if she did not grasp his idea and act quickly, she would be in as great a danger as he was. But however hard he tried, he could see no other way.

The Saint's gaze travelled to the cigaret box on the table and on to the chair beside Cartwright before returning to Emma. Twice more he repeated the message. Emma inclined her head a fraction to show she understood. Slowly she rose and crossed towards the table.

"Sit down!" Cartwright was no longer able to hide the nervousness in his voice.

Emma ignored him. She picked out a cigaret and took her time lighting it, coughing as the smoke hit her lungs. She walked over to the chair next to the window and sat down.

The Saint's eyes indicated a heavy silver statuette that stood on the side table at her elbow. He admired the cool way she had played her part, and his hopes of success began to rise. He looked at his watch again and smiled at Cartwright.

"I don't think he's coming, sonny boy. I really don't. Two minutes to the half hour, Cartwright."

The agent tried to maintain his mask of indifference but the cracks were beginning to show. He left the window and walked back to the centre of the room, ignoring the girl behind him. He looked down at the Saint with a half sneer twisting his lips.

"If anything does happen, Templar, you won't be around to watch it."

Simon seemed to consider the threat and dismiss it from his mind.

"It takes a special kind of toughness to shoot a helpless man,

Cartwright, to look in his face as you pull the trigger, especially when you know that by doing it you're signing your own death warrant."

Cartwright's response was a short scornful laugh, almost a snort, but the Saint's keen ear detected a hollow ring to it, and he kept on jabbing at the signs of weakness.

"You're on your own now. Curdon's run off with the first prize and left you with the wooden spoon. How do you think you're going to get out of this, even if you stay alive long enough to try? You're already a dead man and you'll find that however much they paid you, it won't be enough. The Reds won't want you, and D16 isn't exactly a friendly society. The moment your bosses in Whitehall hear about Curdon and the professor there'll be a contract out on you and nowhere in the world you can run to. Your time's up, Cartwright—now or later, it doesn't matter."

The Saint could see his words hitting home as he spoke them, tearing at the last shreds of the other's self-control. He looked past Cartwright to Emma. She seemed almost hypnotised by his speech, and he thought that his final gamble had failed.

Cartwright moved nearer, using the motion to try to mask the trembling of his muscles. Simon looked into the blackness of the gun muzzle and waited for the crash that heralds oblivion.

It had to happen sometime. There had been too many gambles, too many risks and half chances, and the Saint had always been prepared to die as he had lived, defiant and with a smile on his lips. But now there was a sour taste in his mouth. The scene was wrong, there was something sordid in calmly waiting to die at the hands of a man for whom he felt only contempt.

The Saint tensed himself for the final leap that could have only one outcome, and Cartwright's knuckle whitened on the trigger.

Cartwright was standing directly in front of the Saint, and

neither of them saw Emma move. The statuette slammed into the agent's shoulder, jerking his arm wide as the shot went off.

The Saint sprang in the same instant, catapulting himself forward as the bullet smacked into the wall behind him. His arms closed around Cartwright's legs as the automatic coughed again, harmlessly. As Cartwright fell, the Saint released his hold and turned the dive into a somersault, his palms touching the floor just long enough to send him rolling forward.

Cartwright wriggled aside, his gun hand swinging around. But the Saint was already on his feet, and he jumped forward and brought his heel down on the agent's wrist, pinning it to the floor. Almost casually he bent down and wrenched the gun from Cartwright's grasp, flicking on the safety catch and sliding it into his hip pocket.

He stepped back to allow Cartwright the freedom to move. "Stand up."

The man remained lying on the floor, rubbing his wrist. Simon grabbed his collar and yanked him to his feet. Cartwright was beaten, a whimpering shell of his former self, but the Saint felt no pity. He remembered the face of the sailor and a promise he had made to himself and now intended to keep.

The fight was one-sided and brutal. Cartwright had gone through the standard unarmed combat training, but the instructors had never prepared him to face Simon Templar's anger. The Saint's attack was scientific, calculated to inflict the maximum pain without permitting the welcome relief of unconsciousness. Cartwright tried to fight back but his spirit was broken, and finally the Saint's desire for retribution was appeased. He had found little pleasure in the exercise, only a growing contempt for his victim. His fist travelled at last in a savage uppercut that threatened to separate head and shoulders, and Cartwright collapsed and lay motionless at his feet.

Simon ran a hand through his hair to restore it to some order, and he turned to Emma.

"You throw a mean statue," he remarked appreciatively. "Only next time don't leave it quite so late."

"I'm not as used to this sort of thing as you are," she said shakily. "Do you really think he would have shot you?"

"I have a feeling he was giving it serious consideration," said the Saint. "Now we don't have much time. Phone Inspector Lebeau at the Préfecture and tell him what's happened."

He was already at the door before he finished speaking.

"But where are you going?"

"To the aero club. There's still a chance I can stop them."

12

Simon ran back through the dining room, the way he had come, and out onto the lawn. He was halfway through the belt of trees when he almost stumbled over the body of Cartwright's chauffeur. The man lay on his side, one arm across his face where he had tried to defend himself. A red stain was spreading from an ugly gash above his ear.

A movement behind the tree next to him sent the Saint leaping aside, spinning around as he did so, his arms at half stretch in front of his body to meet an attack. He stared in disbelief as Gaby emerged from his hiding place with a heavy spanner still clutched in his hand.

Simon relaxed and came down off his toes. He looked from the sleeping man to the taxi driver.

"You did that?" It was more a complimentary statement than a question.

Gaby nodded.

"I was coming to the villa to see what had happened to you, and I found him spying on the helicopter."

Simon knelt down and quickly checked that the man still lived.

"You're lucky he has a thick skull, *mon ami,* or you might have committed your first homicide."

"Then he will be all right?" There was genuine relief in the other's voice.

The Saint grinned reassuringly.

"Yes, I should think so, but I wouldn't care to have his headache when he wakes up. The police will be here soon. I want you to go to the villa—you'll find a young lady there. Tell her about this one, and look after her till the flicks arrive."

Without waiting to see his order obeyed, the Saint sprinted the last twenty yards to the clearing. The pilot started his rotors as soon as he saw the Saint emerge from the trees, and had the craft in the air before asking their destination.

In clipped sentences Simon gave him a rundown on the situation as the pilot headed back towards Mandelieu.

The Saint took the observer's binoculars from their case and scanned the long columns of cars beneath them as they flew low over Cannes. The streets were choked with traffic, and his hopes began to rise as he calculated the delays the car he was looking for would have encountered.

They were turning inland from La Napoule before he spotted their quarry. The Mercedes was a silver flake in the distance swinging through the gates of the aerodrome.

By the time the helicopter crossed the perimeter fence the car had passed the row of hangars and stopped beside a twin-engine Beechcraft. Curdon and Maclett were already hurrying to board it. Simon pointed the pilot towards the plane, shouting above the clatter of the rotor blades.

"Can you block their take-off?"

The pilot nodded, his face grim with concentration as he put the helicopter into a steep dive aimed directly towards the plane as it turned to taxi along the runway.

The Saint could clearly see Curdon in the copilot's seat. Maclett's face was pressed against a cabin porthole, looking up curiously at the swiftly descending helicopter.

The chopper skimmed over the length of the plane, its runners missing it by inches. As they shot past, the pilot banked his machine and brought it lower as he did so, and headed back, flying directly towards the taxiing Beechcraft on a set collision course.

The two machines raced towards each other. The ground flashed beneath the helicopter at fantastic speed only a few feet below, and the Saint paid silent tribute to the pilot's skill and nerve. He was already bracing himself for the crash when the pilot pushed the stick forward and sent them zooming upwards so close to the plane that Simon could see the terror in the pilot's eyes.

The Beechcraft slewed to the left a split second before the helicopter started its climb as the pilot desperately tried to avoid a crash, but he was clearly competent for he soon corrected the maneuver and had the plane back on course and halfway towards take-off point before the helicopter could turn and come down again.

The helicopter quickly made up the distance, swooping down on the plane like a falcon onto its prey, hovering directly above it and making lift-off impossible. The plane slowed as the end of the runway drew nearer, weaving left and right across the tarmac strip in a frantic attempt to shake off the pursuit, but the helicopter countered each move with ease.

The plane swung around in a lurching turn and began to head back towards the hangars. The helicopter skimmed over it and came even lower, flying directly in front of it. The plane slowed and the helicopter pilot reduced his speed accordingly, so that the distance between them remained the same.

Simon's attention was focussed on Curdon, who had released his seat belt and was fumbling with the door catch. Suddenly the door flew open and he almost fell out of the plane, a wild grab saving him at the last moment. The pilot cut back the engines to steady the craft, and Curdon held on with one hand as he tried to aim an automatic with the other.

The scream of the engines drowned the sound of the shots, and the Saint had no way of knowing whether they had hit the helicopter or gone wide. The helicopter skimmed from side to side as the pilot did everything he could to make himself harder to hit while still managing to maintain the same speed and height.

Simon looked along the runway and saw the flashing lights of a convoy of police cars racing through the aerodrome gates. The single column became two as they fanned out on either side of the runway. Two cars overtook the rest, sweeping to a screeching halt behind the Beechcraft and making a further double-back impossible.

Without warning, the helicopter's engine coughed and spluttered and it veered to the right. The pilot fought to bring the machine back on course, but its controls seemed to only half respond. He looked at the Saint and shook his head.

"Something hit us. . . . We must go down."

"Just put me as close as you can."

The pilot wrenched the helicopter to the left so that they were sinking squarely ahead of the approaching plane. The Beechcraft skidded to a sideways stop as its pilot jammed on the brakes.

As the helicopter came to ground, the Saint jumped the last few feet, landing on his toes and sprinting across the tarmac towards the plane, bent almost double against the buffeting air from the flailing rotor blades and zigzagging like a rugby winger as bullets ricocheted off the runway and flew past him.

The plane and helicopter were now in the center of a ring of cars behind which the police were quickly taking up their positions but holding fire for fear of hitting the Saint.

The Saint ducked under the plane's nose, coming around to the pilot's side out of Curdon's line of fire. He reached up and yanked open the door with one hand as his other grasped the pilot's coat and pulled him bodily out of the plane. Curdon turned and fired as the pilot toppled onto the runway and no longer obstructed his aim, but the Saint had been expecting a shot and ducked below the fuselage.

He had noticed Emma and Gaby in the back of the leading police car as the helicopter had landed. As he flattened himself against the Beechcraft, he saw Emma duck under the taxi driver's restraining arm and start to run across the no man's land between the police cordon and the plane.

Maclett, who had been watching from the safety of the cabin, moved with surprising speed as soon as he saw his daughter and recognised the danger she was in. He threw himself forward directly between Curdon and the Saint, shouting to his daughter as he did so.

"Emma, stop!"

But the girl did not hear and was already at the edge of the runway.

Maclett was trying to climb out of the plane, but Curdon grabbed his shoulder and dragged him back into the pilot's seat with his gun aimed straight at the professor's chest. He gestured towards the pilot, who was now getting gingerly to his feet on the ground.

"Get him back on board, Templar!"

Simon looked from Maclett to Curdon and shook his head.

"You wouldn't kill the golden goose, old boy."

For a moment the three men stared at each other as each sought his own way to break the deadlock.

Emma reached Simon's side before he could stop her. She came to a halt in front of the open door, suddenly rigid with fear as she realised the danger.

Curdon took a direct aim at her.

"I'll kill her right enough. Stay right where you are, Miss Maclett."

The professor stepped forward, but Curdon moved to one side so that he could keep both father and daughter covered. Maclett's voice shook with despair and surprise.

"What kind of man are you?"

Curdon ignored him.

"Listen to me, Templar. The pilot gets back in and we take off unmolested, or—"

"No!" Maclett sprang forward, clawing at the gun and knocking Curdon off balance.

The automatic fired into the air, the detonation ear-shattering in the confined space.

The two men wrestled in the doorway, half in, half out of the plane, and the Saint took advantage of the diversion to reach the other side of the cabin. He vaulted into the plane, one arm locking around Curdon's throat, the other pinning his gun hand to his side.

Maclett released his hold and jumped down beside his daughter as the Saint gathered all his strength into one titanic heave that threw Curdon clear out of the plane. The gun flew from his grip as he crashed onto the runway with barely enough wind left to crawl to his knees.

Curdon's hate-filled eyes blazed up at the Saint, the voice a rasping sob.

"Ten years ago I'd have taken you . . . you . . ."

Slowly, almost comically, Curdon pitched forward and lay still, face down on the warm tarmac.

The Saint raised a sardonic eyebrow.

"I always like a gallant loser," he remarked, to no attentive audience.

He watched as two policemen dragged Curdon to their car, and then turned and walked over to the plane where Maclett, Emma, and Lebeau were waiting.

Simon gave Lebeau a mocking bow, and held out his wrists as if inviting the handcuffs.

"A pleasure to meet you again, Inspector. Am I under arrest?"

Lebeau shook his head.

"Not exactly, but it would not be to your advantage to prolong this stay in Cannes."

"Forty-eight hours?"

"That is exactly the time it will take me to decide what charges are to be answered. Now if you will excuse me I have some pressing matters to attend to. The British Government has already been making some extraordinary representations to Paris about this affair."

"Then there'll surely be a lot of lovely forms to fill out," Simon prophesied.

When the detective had left them the Saint studied the professor. Maclett's shoulders drooped and he looked as if he had aged ten years in a few hours. Emma was holding his arm, but he refused to meet her eyes.

"You wouldn't have been free, Daddy. They were just going to use you and keep your work for themselves."

"Aye."

"I think there may be a way to sort things out, Professor," Simon ventured. "Depending on how you feel."

Maclett looked up with some of the old fire returning to his eyes.

"I feel like a damn fool."

"Which is the beginning of wisdom," said the Saint.

13

The Palais des Festivals was packed to overflowing, with scientists making up only a part of the audience. News of Maclett's adventure had made headlines around the world, and photographers and reporters vied with ordinary sensation-seekers for the best seats.

Maclett stood alone in the center of the dais, a lectern before him and a huge blackboard covered with the hieroglyphics of chemical equations behind. He closed his folder of notes and moved aside from the lectern.

"That is the basic premise as it will be published by Her

Majesty's Government. The rest you are free to work out for yourselves—if you can."

The hall rang with the applause, and in the wings Simon smiled at Emma and nodded towards the exit.

"Let's leave your father to enjoy his moment of glory alone."

As they walked away from the Palais, Emma asked: "Why did you rush off from the airfield yesterday?"

"Being a loyal taxpayer and realising that our friend Willie was likely to have a good deal of government expense money in the villa, not to mention whatever the Russians had paid him in advance, I felt it my duty to ensure its safety."

The girl stopped, looking at him accusingly.

"You mean you stole it?"

The Saint laughed.

"Let's just say I believe in making sure that good deeds are properly rewarded and so now does Gaby. He'll probably start up his own fleet of taxis with his share."

A little farther west he steered her away from the Croisette, up the Rue Commandant André.

"Where are we going?"

"To Mère Besson's, the best Provençal restaurant on this coast, for the best meal she can provide, courtesy of Sir William."

Emma snuggled against his shoulder.

"I don't know how I'm ever going to thank you for what you did," she said.

The Saint smiled and put an arm around her.

"Don't worry," he said. "Between us, we'll probably think of something."

II

The Red Sabbath

1

A fine drizzle blurred the sharp outlines of the sprawling pile of concrete and glass boxes that is Heathrow Airport. The midday sun was hidden by a low canopy of grey-black cloud. A brisk breeze lifted the litter of empty cigaret packets and assorted paper wrappings that are a feature of most British public places and skimmed them across the desolate expanse of runways and cargo yards.

The plane taxied slowly to a halt, shuddering slightly as the engine died. Simon Templar wiped the mist from the window, and grinned wryly as he surveyed the dismal scene.

"Oh to be in London, now that autumn's here."

"I beg your pardon?"

He turned to the middle-aged matron in the next seat who was trying to untangle her portly frame from the confines of her safety belt. She had spoken little during the flight from Nice, and he had been extremely grateful for her taciturnity. There was an aura surrounding such heavily powdered and perfumed dowagers which he found conducive to claustrophobia.

"I said it's good to be back."

The woman ceased her struggles and regarded him with an expression that was a mixture of amazement and concern.

"If you think that, young man, then I can only conclude that the Riviera sun has been too strong for your brain."

He laughed and reached across and released the clasp of her seat belt. She spared him a final parting frown before heaving her bulk upright and pushing her way into the file of passengers inching their way along the aisle.

He was not surprised at her reaction. London is a city that is either loved or loathed; it brooks no indifference. It has been compared to hell and it has also been said that when a man is tired of London he is tired of life. Simon Templar placed himself squarely in the latter camp.

He could appreciate London because he was able to compare it with most of the other great cities of the world. It was true that he had seen more beautiful ones, admired the splendour of more ancient ones, relaxed in the serenity of more peaceful ones, and fought in more violent ones, but only in London did the individual characteristics that make other cities interesting merge together to form one unique entity.

It was the one spot on the globe that he truly regarded as home. It had been the scene of some of the most memorable episodes in his swashbuckling career, and in his more reflective moments he sometimes wondered if it would be the backdrop to his last.

Not, it should be stated, that he believed that day to be imminent. As he strolled leisurely into the arrival terminal he had no more nefarious intention in mind than a change of clothes and dinner with a friend about whose identity he was not in the least particular, as long as her eyes reflected the candlelight, her hair shone and curled, and her shape curved in the correct places and proportions.

At passport control, the man at the desk said nothing, but simply glanced at the Saint, then at the picture, flicked over the pages, and handed the book back with a look that said "I know who you are and so something must be wrong, but I can't find it."

He waited with the rest of the passengers until the baggage arrived. Most of them were returning from holiday; and if any recognised the tall tanned man in their midst they did not, in true British fashion, make the fact obvious, even though all but the most myopic must have seen those same clear blue eyes smiling at them from the front page of every French newspaper less than forty-eight hours before. He retrieved his suitcase and walked through to the customs hall. A British passport clearly states that Her Britannic Majesty requires all whom it may concern to allow the bearer to pass freely, without let or hindrance. This does not however apply to the said Britannic Majesty's customs officers, who, like the Ancient Mariner, stoppeth one in three. The Saint looked along the line of people ahead of him in the queue and was already resigned to his fate before he lifted his suitcase onto the counter.

He studied the list held before him and gravely considered each item.

"No. No. No. Certainly not. Also I'm afraid I've spent all my counterfeit coins, smoked the last of my opium, and all my meat and poultry is fully cooked."

The officer gave him a look which placed him somewhere in the lower regions of the insect world.

"Open the case, please, sir."

He opened the case and watched as the contents were riffled. The official searched with professional diligence, and only when he was convinced that every shirt had been creased did he close the lid and scrawl his mark across it.

"Thank you, sir."

Only a well-trained British civil servant can make a statement of gratitude sound like an insult. The Saint bestowed his most dazzling smile upon him and moved on to merge with the procession flowing out to join the crowd of waiting friends and messengers in the main concourse.

He had not covered a dozen yards before he felt rather than heard the two men behind him. His instinct for danger was so finely honed by years of living on a knife's edge that he sensed their approach even among the crush of people around him. He stopped so abruptly that the two men had to swerve to avoid cannoning into him. He turned on his heel.

"Okay, brothers, and what can I do for you?"

"Brothers" was an apt description, for the two men facing him could easily have shared the same parents. Both were tall and powerfully built, their expensively tailored light grey suits failing to hide the breadth of their shoulders or the slight bulge beneath their left arms. The only real difference was the colour of their hair, one blond, the other a jet black, but this dissimilarity had been reduced by the close-cropped style they both affected. Despite the overcast sky their eyes were hidden behind dark glasses.

The Saint put down his case and stood with his arms hanging loosely by his sides, as deceptively relaxed as a coiled snake.

The blond man spoke first.

"Mr. Templar?"

"Me? No, sorry. McFiggin's the name."

The dark-haired twin bent and read the tag on his suitcase. He nodded to his companion.

"Come with us, please."

As he spoke, the man lifted the case and made a move towards the exit. The Saint's hand flashed out, fingers of steel gripping his arm and staying him in mid-stride.

The Saint's voice was soft and reasonable.

"Now hold it. What is this? Who are you?"

The dark-haired man made no attempt to return the case, and the Saint felt the muscles beneath his grasp tighten.

"We have orders to collect you."

"Orders? From whom?"

The blond man stepped between them, looking around quickly as if the delay worried him.

"Shh. Please, no fuss, Mr. Templar."

The Saint's tone was conversational but his words were edged with a menace neither man could fail to appreciate.

"Fuss? You tell me what is going on, or I'll raise the roof clean off this airport."

"Our orders are simply to collect you, not to explain. You are needed urgently in a confidential matter."

"By whom?"

The blond man's voice fell to a whisper.

"Colonel Leon Garvi."

The revelation of the identity of his would-be host told the Saint many things, not least the reason for the two men's caution. Slowly he released his grip.

"All right," he said quietly. "Lead on."

The blond man carried his case, and the Saint followed him out of the building, while his colleague walked a few paces behind, his eyes constantly scanning the surrounding area, his hand resting lightly on the top button of his jacket.

Outside the terminal they stopped by a blue Volvo that had been left in the middle of a No Parking zone. A few yards away a policeman scowled impotently at the small CD badge beside the rear number plate. The blond man put the case in the trunk and slid in behind the wheel while the other joined the Saint in the back. Neither man appeared inclined to volunteer any further information, and Simon did not press them.

He used the drive into town to run through all he knew of Colonel Leon Garvi.

They had met a couple of times in the past, first in Tel Aviv and later in Zurich, and on both occasions he had had the opportunity of watching the colonel at work and had developed a deep respect for his abilities. Garvi was a born hunter, and his quarry was invariably human. He had gained his reputation tracking down war criminals before turning his attention to terrorists. His name never appeared in official reports or the newspapers, but he was famed and feared in those circles in which he chose to move. It was said that he never failed to find the man he sought, and he was held in almost supernatural awe both by those who feared him and those who served him.

Simon could think of no reason why Garvi should want to see him, but he knew that the explanation when it came would be an interesting one. The Saint had no qualms about accepting the invitation. He had long ago ceased to question the vagaries of fate. He had followed the promise of adventure to Cannes and had not been disappointed; that the prospect of mayhem should present itself so soon did not surprise him. Things happened to him not only because he looked for them, but because he brazenly expected them. He had set his feet on the road to adventure and was prepared to make room and find time for it wherever and whenever it appeared, taking every moment as it came.

At that particular moment he was being chauffeured to London, which was where he wanted to go and in a vehicle that was more comfortable than the taxi he would otherwise have taken. He asked for no more.

Outside, the factories flashed by in a blur of smoky dullness. Beyond them, the neat and tidy streets of suburbia stretched in orderly ranks into the far distance. As they drew nearer the centre, blocks of fading Victorian terraces replaced the smart semis until they were cruising through Hammersmith towards Kensington.

They crawled along Kensington High Street between the tall blocks of department stores and pavements overflowing with shoppers and harassed office workers in search of tea and sandwiches, finally turning into Palace Green and stopping outside the Israeli embassy.

He was taken in by a secondary entrance, through elaborate security precautions which cannot be detailed here, to the third floor where a single door led from a small reception area. Beside it, a mountain of a man sat behind a desk. The blond man smiled a greeting that was not returned.

"Mr. Templar."

The mountain pressed a button on the console in front of him, and almost immediately a green light flashed above the door. The blond man held it open and the Saint walked through.

The inner office was long and narrow and ultrafunctional. One wall was entirely taken up by banks of filing cabinets, the other by maps which hung from ceiling to floor and were covered in a multitude of tiny colored flags. Garvi sat behind an expanse of leather-topped desk at the far end, and through the windows behind it Simon could see the tops of the trees in Kensington Gardens. There was a deceptive air of peace about the room, and he did not care to shatter it by thinking of the actions that might have been planned within its walls.

Garvi rose as the Saint approached, smiling and stretching out his hand. He was in his mid-fifties, tall with the supple strength of a big cat. His steel-grey hair was cut cleanly around the ears and neck, and his face was lean and tanned. But the most dominant of his features were the eyes. They had an almost hypnotic appeal, as if they were capable of penetrating a man's brain and reading his innermost thoughts.

"Simon, it's good to see you again."

They shook hands, and the Saint smiled.

"And you, Colonel. It's been a longish time."

"Too long. Please sit down."

"What do you want to see me about? Your men were very insistent."

He was aware that the blond man had followed him into the room and was leaning against the door. Garvi nodded towards him.

"This is Yakovitz, one of my top operatives. He will be helping you."

"Helping me do what, Leon? What's this all about?"

"R.S."

The Saint's eyes narrowed. He had heard of the Arab "Red Sabbath" organization, but then who capable of reading a paper or listening to a news broadcast had not? They had bombed and machine-gunned their way into the headlines in a raid on a kibbutz three years before, and since then had never been out of them for long. They claimed to be fighting a holy war that would destroy the state of Israel. Their weapons were terror, and their victims the weak and the defenceless and the innocent. A school bus blown apart, an airport departure lounge machine-gunned, aircraft hijacked and passengers held for ransom. They were the worst kind of enemy to fight—unpredictable fanatics, prepared, even eager, to die for their cause.

Garvi continued.

"One of their top men, Abdul Hakim, has defected."

"So?"

"He's here in London. We are after him, Simon, but so far—no luck. We think he's heading for South America, but that he's been held up, maybe through lack of money, passport, visa, we don't know, but we have got to find him."

The Saint began to see the first strands of the web that was being spun around him.

"Sorry."

"What?"

"I'm not heading any murder squad, Leon."

Garvi's reassuring smile never reached his eyes.

"No, no, you don't understand. We need him alive. This is their first defection. He knows all their top men. Don't you see what that information could do for us? We could destroy the whole group! This man is deep underground, his own people are after him too, they want to try and silence him before we get to him. He's buried himself in the city jungle—a jungle that you know like the back of your hand. Right?"

The Saint was hesitant.

"Right."

"Well, Tel Aviv has drafted in one of our top counterterrorist officers, Captain Zabin, to track him down. But the captain doesn't know London. Now do you see? We want you as a guide, Simon."

The Saint was still unconvinced.

"This man's a killer. So if we catch up with him he's going to shoot it out, isn't he?"

Garvi shook his head slowly, as if the action alone would dispel the Saint's doubts.

"I know what you're thinking, but you must believe me. I respect this city as much as you do. If there is shooting, it will not be from us. I have given strict orders. My solemn word. Will you help us?"

His eyes searched the Saint's face as if trying to read the answer before it was spoken.

Simon recalled the pictures he had seen of twisted bodies in shattered buildings, of young lives sacrificed to a hate they did not understand.

Slowly he nodded.

Garvi visibly relaxed, and the Saint realised what an effort it had cost him to ask the aid of an outsider.

"Thank you."

He looked beyond the Saint to Yakovitz.

"Ask Captain Zabin to come in."

Simon heard the door open, and rose to greet the officer. And a look of total astonishment replaced the bland expression of polite cordiality into which he had conventionally composed his features.

2

Captain Zabin stopped a yard away, and seemed almost as startled as the Saint.

She wore a military-style blouse and knee-length pleated skirt, but even the severely functional line of her clothes could not completely mask a figure that undulated in all the right places. Her smooth skin was tinged with a light tan, her features delicate but conveying a subtle strength. Like Garvi's, her eyes shone with a strange, disquieting intenseness. Her black hair was brushed back and fastened by a tortoise-shell clip at the nape of her neck.

She eyed the Saint with undisguised disapproval, and looked questioningly at her superior.

"Is this the man?"

The colonel grinned.

"Captain Leila Zabin, allow me to introduce Simon Templar."

She made no attempt to conceal her disappointment.

"From what you told me, I was expecting someone much more . . ."

As she faltered, the Saint stepped forward, smiling as his eyes flickered over her body in candid approval.

"Me too, Captain. But who's grumbling?" he murmured. "Simon Templar, at your service."

The ringing of the telephone split a stillness that threatened to become uncomfortable.

Garvi lifted the transreceiver, listened for a few moments, and then replaced it. He turned back to the Saint and shrugged an apology.

"Simon, I'm sorry, but I have to go. In any case there is little more I can tell you. Captain Zabin will give you any additional information you may require. Here is the file on Hakim. The first thing you must do is set up a base away from the embassy. Let me know as soon as you have chosen a convenient place."

They shook hands, and Simon waited until Garvi had left before turning to Leila.

"Well," he said, "let's get started."

Leila hesitated.

"Where are we going?"

"To set up our base as the good colonel told us."

She made to bar his way but he sidestepped past her. Yakovitz still leant against the door and showed no indication of moving. For a moment their eyes met, and almost as if a telepathic message passed between them the blond man stepped aside and allowed them through into the reception lobby.

"Come along. I'll give you directions as we drive."

Leila and Yakovitz had no alternative but to follow, but as he descended the stairs he felt their eyes scorching the back of his head and smiled.

The Volvo was still outside, but there was no sign of the dark-haired chauffeur. As Yakovitz walked towards the driver's door the Saint laid a restraining hand on his arm.

"I'll drive."

Yakovitz looked questioningly at Leila, who replied with a shrug of indifference. Reluctantly he handed over the keys.

The Saint guided the car through the Kensington traffic towards Knightsbridge.

"Is this the first time you've been to London, Captain?"

"Yes."

"You must allow me to give you a guided tour."

"Thank you, Mr. Templar, but I think not. We are here on business, not on holiday."

"Your loss, Leila. Still, I have a feeling you'll be seeing quite a bit of it even if it is on business."

He shot the car between a bus and a taxi with an inch to spare on either wing, smiling at the Anglo-Saxon epithets that flowed from both sides.

"You said that Hakim's own men are hunting him. Do we know anything about them?"

He sensed Leila's relief that the conversation had returned to business, and wondered at the brittle quality of her screen of toughness.

"All we are certain of is that three of them arrived as seamen yesterday on a freighter at the West India Dock. We're not sure, but we believe one of them is a man named Masrouf. He and Hakim were in on the start of the R.S."

Simon nosed the Volvo into the stream of traffic negotiating Hyde Park Corner.

"So he'd know where to go looking while we run around in circles?"

"You are here to make sure that we don't," she said coldly.

"Let's get this straight. An Arab terrorist is somewhere in London. A handful of gunmen are looking for him so that they can help him on his way to Allah. We are also turning over the paving stones hoping something will crawl out. All good fun—but where does British Intelligence come into all this?"

"They don't. This is a private affair."

He laughed as he pictured the scene that would be enacted in offices in Scotland Yard and Whitehall once their activities became known.

"I don't think the Special Branch would agree with you."

"My concern is Abdul Hakim—not your Special Branch, your D16, or your government."

Simon spun the wheel and turned into Upper Brook Street, screeching under the radiator of a Rolls and almost giving the ducal personage in the back apoplexy.

In a few moments he slowed and turned into a small courtyard behind the buildings that fronted the thoroughfare, braking outside a mews terrace converted to whitewashed two-storey houses. Before he had switched off the engine, Yakovitz was out of the car, his eyes darting from window to window.

Leila considered the house with the same disapproving frown with which she had greeted the Saint. Simon unlocked the front door and led the way inside.

They entered directly into a long, open-plan lounge, with an iron spiral staircase rising from the centre of the room to connect with the bedrooms above. It was furnished with the miscellaneous mementoes collected in years of wandering to every part of the world, and might have given an interior designer palpitations had not each individual piece carried the unmistakeable stamp of its owner's good taste.

Leila shook her head.

"Very nice. You live well. But hardly the place for an operational headquarters."

"Exactly, which makes it ideal. Of course, if you prefer, we could always advertise by hanging out the Israeli flag."

"I do not find your humour appropriate, Mr. Templar. I would not have chosen such a place, but for the present I must accept your argument."

She turned to Yakovitz, who had stayed in the doorway watching the street.

"Do what you have to."

The agent unlocked the car trunk and brought out a small metal detector and began to systematically scan the walls.

"Most professional, but really quite unnecessary," Simon remarked. "The house isn't bugged."

Leila ignored him, and wandered over to the collection of weapons displayed above the fireplace. They were a strange assortment of deadly instruments that ranged from a Zulu assegai to a harpoon gun, taking in a staggering variety of firearms on the way. She removed a kukri and carefully tested its sharpness with her thumb.

"You keep an impressive arsenal, Mr. Templar."

He took the knife from her and replaced it with a chuckle.

"I hope you're not superstitious, Captain. They say that a kukri should never be drawn unless blood is shed." He waved his hand to encompass the collection. "Weapons I have not been killed with. Some day I'll tell you the stories behind them. Now, shall we christen the new headquarters?"

Leila turned to face him.

"Mr. Templar, let us get one thing quite straight. I am in command here. You are the guide. Is that clear?"

He walked over to a side table and considered the bottles that covered it.

"Now let me guess—vodka?"

She could not quite master the anger in her voice.

"I don't drink. Did you hear me, Mr. Templar?"

"I heard you, Captain. Now why don't you check in with Garvi while your friend brings in the cases. There are only two bedrooms, so Yakowatsit here will have to kip on the couch. Unless of course we can think of an alternative idea."

Again his gaze travelled the length of her body and he was pleased at the flush of embarrassment it brought. It was the first strictly female emotion she had shown.

"That arrangement will be perfectly suitable."

While she telephoned and Yakovitz carried the cases upstairs, Simon relaxed on the soft leather couch and flicked through the folder Garvi had given him. Most of the information simply documented Hakim's terrorist activities, his personal appearance and habits, and was of little use as far as their current job was concerned. More important were the two photographs. They showed a man of about thirty with crinkly black hair and a Zapata moustache, who even on film managed to convey a feeling of tension and danger. One was a straight head and shoulders picture, the other a snap of him taken on a rooftop with an attractive girl about ten years his junior.

Simon was still studying it when Leila finished her call and joined him.

"Colonel Garvi approves of your choice," she said with visible reluctance. "He appears to place great trust in you, Mr. Templar. But I must ask you to take this operation more seriously. I do not know if it is a defence mechanism because I am a woman, but I find your attitude to this important mission"—she searched her vocabulary for a correct word—"slap-happy? You have scarcely looked at that file. Instead of being concerned with drinks and . . . er . . . sleeping accommodation, you should be deciding where our search should begin."

The Saint removed the picture and tossed the rest of the contents of the folder on the table as he rose. He affected surprise at her comments.

"Oh, that? I thought that was obvious."

"Obvious?"

"The snapshot of him in London."

She took the photograph from him and considered it carefully.

"That is London? How can you tell?"

He pointed to a small rectangle on the far left of the frame.

"The tower at Kings Cross station."

"Oh! We thought it was a chimney pot."

The Saint clicked his tongue in mock reproof.

"How very . . . er . . . slap-happy of you, Captain."

He took a large-scale map of inner London from the bureau and spread it out on the table.

"Now the Kings Cross tower is on the far left, so if we draw a line along the Euston Road we have one boundary."

His finger stubbed at the map.

"There's a church there, but no sign of the steeple in the photograph. Therefore we can rule out the area east of Farringdon Street. There's no natural third boundary, so we'll have to join up the two extremes."

He drew a line from Holborn Viaduct diagonally across the map to link up with the station.

"The sun is high, therefore the picture was taken from the west. And judging by the smallness of it in the picture, the tower is a fair way in the distance, which means we can eliminate these."

He shaded in the roads immediately before Kings Cross. A small triangle of about a dozen major roads and twice as many side streets remained.

"The picture was taken somewhere within that area," he said, "so I suggest we start looking there. The photograph is three years old, so it's a long shot, but it's the best lead we have at the moment."

Leila smiled for the first time since they had met.

"Very efficient, Mr. Templar. I am impressed."

The Saint half bowed.

"All part of the service, Captain. Now I too must make a telephone call."

He dialled, and drummed his fingers on the desk top until his ring was answered.

"Hullo, Harry. This is the Saint. I've got a job for you. The mark's a bloke called Hakim, and somebody's doing him a ticket. I want to know who. Also he may be trying to buy a persuader. Three other sheikhs who want to talk to him might be asking questions as well. I want everything you can get, but particularly the I.D. of the inkman. A couple of ponies for starters, and I'll raise you if it's official. Yes, I know it's a tall one. No, I'm not expecting miracles. Just do your best. I'll see you in the usual at ten."

He had been watching Leila while he talked, and had seen her expression change from admiration to suspicion.

"Who was that?"

"An acquaintance of mine, one Harry-the-Nose. Not the sort of chap one takes home to mummy, but has a lot of friends and may be able to save us some time."

"And do you usually talk to your acquaintances in code?"

For a moment her meaning escaped him; and then, as the light dawned, he laughed.

"Code! Yes I suppose that's really what it is when you stop to think about it. The trouble with you is that the English you've been taught is too perfect. Only BBC announcers ac-tu-ally speak like that," he mimicked. "That wasn't code I was speaking in–it was jargon. In his own field Harry is a professional, and just like any other professional–lawyers, stockbrokers, doctors, or whatever–he uses a different language. All I told him was that Hakim was looking for someone to forge him a passport. I asked him to find out who, and I also mentioned that he might be trying to obtain a firearm and that three other Arabs were enquiring as to his whereabouts."

"And the horse?"

"The horse? Oh, you mean the ponies, that's his fee. Fifty pounds."

"I'm sorry I doubted you," Leila said, almost sheepishly.

"Think nothing of it," Simon said cheerfully.

He folded the map and slipped it into his pocket. From a corner cabinet he took a powerful pair of binoculars.

"Okay, let's go."

"Go?" she echoed. "Go where?"

The Saint smiled.

"I'm taking you to church," he said.

3

Leaving Yakovitz to take any calls, the Saint and Leila drove back towards Hyde Park Corner, turning down Constitution Hill and onto the broad red carpet of the Mall.

The rain had stopped, and a watery afternoon sun was managing to break through the clouds. Leila's head was turned towards the Saint, but her gaze travelled past him as she took in the splendour of Buckingham Palace and its scarlet-tunicked guardsmen, and the elegant lines of the Mall's Georgian terraces with their tall windows and stately white columns. Ahead of them, Admiralty Arch straddled the road, and through its gateway she could see the lions and fountains grouped at the foot of Nelson's Column.

As they became enmeshed in the traffic clogging Trafalgar Square, she turned to the Saint and smiled.

"You live in a beautiful city, Simon."

There was a new warmth to her voice, and he was glad to note that another barrier had been broken down by the use of his first name.

"Yes, it is beautiful. But London isn't just imposing buildings and monuments, it's people. I hope you get the chance to meet some of them."

"So do I. Now please, Simon, just where are we going?"

They were cruising past the Law Courts and entering Fleet Street and he pointed straight ahead.

"There," he said. "St. Paul's Cathedral."

For a while she was silent as she looked up at the black dome with its golden cross that soared above the surrounding offices and shops.

"But why?"

"For the finest view in London. We've narrowed the location of that picture down to a fairly small area, but it's still big enough for a person like Hakim to lose himself in. We can't simply wander around the streets hoping he's going to pop out for a packet of cigarets just as we drive by. I'm hoping that by getting a bird's-eye view we can draw a finer bead on that rooftop."

He left the car near Ludgate Hill, and as they walked up towards the cathedral he pointed out the balconies that encircle the bottom and top of the dome.

"We'll start at the Golden Gallery, that's the one immediately below the cross, and try to get a general fix with the binoculars," he said. "Then we can go down to the Stone Gallery and use the telescopes there to try and pinpoint it more exactly."

Side by side they climbed the sweeping flight of stone steps and entered through the main doors. Leila stopped as she passed beyond the shadows of the portico and was suddenly confronted by the spacious grandeur of the white and gold interior.

"It's magnificent!" she said.

Simon took her arm and led her past the tombs and monuments until they reached the foot of a curving stone staircase cut into the south wall.

"The view is even better from the Whispering Gallery," he said. "But I'm afraid we really can't spend too long looking around."

Leila nodded, but there was genuine regret in her voice. "No, I suppose not."

St. Paul's is 365 feet high and there are 528 steps to the top. The Saint took them two at a time as far as the Whispering Gallery. From there the spiral stone stairway becomes narrower at each turn, and he was forced to bend almost double under the low ceiling. When they finally emerged into the sunlight, even his superbly trained muscles were beginning to protest.

Far below them the streets of London stretched into the distance like the strands of a giant spider's web. The Saint walked slowly around the north side and leant on the stone balustrade as he adjusted the focus of the binoculars. Leila held out the map and photograph so that he could see them without moving the glasses.

"It has to be somewhere between Grays Inn Road and Kings Cross Road. Beyond the Royal Free Hospital and to the east of the church, but not as far as Bryant Street, or the tower would appear much larger."

He was talking more to himself than to Leila, and as he spoke he shaded in more of the map, gradually making the triangle smaller and smaller until only three or four streets remained. Finally he lowered the glasses and rubbed the water from his eyes.

"We're getting closer," he told her. "The trouble is that from this height all the blocks of houses look roughly the same size, but you can see from the photograph that behind the roof they were standing on there's a street of buildings a storey taller. If we can use the telescope to locate one of these roads where the houses are lower than those they back onto, then we've scored a bull's-eye."

Leila was staring out across the skyline, concentrating on the area the Saint had been scanning a few moments before. Her eyes were half closed against the sun, and he could almost feel the tautness of her body. She reminded him of an eagle hovering in the air before swooping on its prey. Her fist clenched, but without crumpling the photograph.

"We must find it," she said. "There is no time to lose."

She turned and led the way back down the stairs, walking around the Whispering Gallery without stopping to admire the view it offered. He followed more slowly, and she was already standing beside the telescopes by the time he again came out into the daylight.

A rapid change had come over her with the prospect of getting closer to her quarry. The sharpness had returned to her voice, and the light he had found so unsettling at their first meeting shone again from her eyes. On the drive from his home, she had mellowed from being a soldier to being a woman; now, just as quickly and unpredictably, she had switched back again. He sensed that there was something more behind her dedication than mere patriotism and a hatred of her country's enemies, something that verged on the fanatical. He had hunted many men, but only a few of them had he truly hated; more than most men he understood the subtle difference between crusade and personal vendetta. At that moment he found Captain Leila Zabin a more interesting enigma than the man they were pursuing.

He angled the telescope and pressed a coin into the slot. The lens cleared to give a needle-sharp view over the rooftops. He was aware of Leila pacing impatiently behind him as he moved the telescope by fractions of a degree until he had studied every inch of the unshaded area on the map.

"Not Caxton Street," he said, letting her share his thoughts as they came to him, "because they're five-storey tenements. And it can't be Swans Court, because they are only two. All the buildings in Alma Street have pitched roofs, so therefore that only leaves Little Claymore or one of the alleys running from it. Yes, that's it, Little Claymore Street. It's got to be."

He straightened and stretched away the cramp from his

shoulders. Leila took the map and located the street for herself.

"Are you sure?" she insisted.

The Saint shrugged.

"No, I'm not absolutely sure, but I'd lay odds on it."

"Good. Let us see if you would win your bet," she said briskly, and turned on her heel to lead the way back.

While it may appear on the map as a sprawling metropolis with no clear-cut boundaries except the river that divides north from south, London is really only a collection of villages that have been squashed together. Like a giant amoeba the city has flowed around and absorbed them but never quite managed to crush their separate identities. Although to the visitor it may seem that only the names remain—Kensington, Camberwell, Hackney, Hampstead and the rest—something of the original still exists in each. Consequently extremes are never far apart, with streets of tenements running into avenues of mansions. Only the villagers are aware of the dividing lines, although they are as real as any national frontier.

Clerkenwell lies on the northern doorstep of the City. It begins less than a mile from the Bank of England, yet for all the resemblance the two districts bear to each other they might as well be on opposite sides of the country.

It is an area of back streets, of small shops and factories. Little Claymore Street is the same as the roads that surround it, a narrow backwater running between banks of decaying terraces. The Victorian villas designed for large middle-class families and their maids have long since been converted into warrens of tiny bed-sitters that mainly provide a cheap roof for the ever shifting population of students and immigrants. The iron railings that line the front steps are rusted and bent, the plaster cracked, and the paint peeling from windows and doors.

"The other face of London," Simon observed as they turned into the street and he slowed the car to a crawl.

Leila made no reply. She was sitting eagerly forward in her

seat, her eyes sweeping the buildings on either side. They were halfway along the street when she grabbed his arm.

"Look!" she exclaimed.

At the far end, a group of men and women were staring up at a third-floor window. Most were Pakistanis, a few West Indians, and whatever was going on behind the drawn curtains had obviously upset them.

"Don't raise your hopes, Leila," he cautioned her. "Lots of things happen every day in an area like this. It could just be an eviction. And if it's not, we may already be too late."

She turned to him, her eyes blazing with irrational anger.

"Can you think of a better place to start?"

"No," he admitted, and eased the car into the kerb.

He had come to find the scene in the photograph and was quite prepared to force his way into every house if necessary. At least this one had its front door already open.

The group of bystanders fell silent and backed away as he and Leila climbed out of the car and ran up the steps and into the hall. The Saint leapt nimbly up the uncarpeted stairs with Leila at his heels. From outside came the prolonged sound of a car horn, and he remembered the new station wagon that had been parked farther along the street and wondered.

As they gained the top landing a woman screamed. Simon reached the door in a single stride and did not bother trying the handle but launched his whole body forward, twisting as he did so. His shoulder smashed into the worm-eaten wood, shattering the lock and sending the door crashing open. His momentum carried him a yard into the room before he could recover his balance. He straightened and stopped in his tracks, his arms held out from his sides to prevent Leila from passing.

A girl sat facing him. Her long black hair was dishevelled, her eyes wide with fear. On her cheek the dark skin still showed the imprint of the hand that had slapped it, and there was an ugly swelling on the side of her chin.

Two dark-skinned men stood on either side of her. Both wore

roll-necked jumpers and jeans, army flak jackets stretched tight across their shoulders. If it came to a fight they would each concede him a couple of inches in height and reach, but would be at no obvious disadvantage as far as weight and muscle were concerned. The Saint looked down the muzzles of the two automatics levelled at his chest and seemed to find something amusing there.

"If you use those popguns," he said calmly, "you'll have to shoot your way out floor by floor. My men are on every landing."

With no way of checking the bluff, the two men hesitated. And then, as if to underline his warning, came the tramp of feet on the stairs as some of the crowd from outside summoned enough courage to find out what was happening.

The smaller and heavier of the two jerked his head towards an open door at the far end of the room, through which the Saint could see the flat rooftop pictured in the photograph. Still keeping their guns trained on the Saint and Leila, they backed towards it. Simon waited until they had reached the roof and disappeared from view around the corner of the house before moving.

He turned to Leila.

"Look after the girl and get rid of the sightseers," he ordered.

"Simon, be careful."

The words followed him without effect as he went through the door by which the two Arabs had departed.

The narrow frontage of the house belied its depth. The girl's room was a former attic directly beneath the pitched roof which was the only one visible from the road. The flat area onto which the two men had run and where the picture had been taken was the top of the remainder of the house, which stretched back until it almost joined the rear of the buildings in the next street.

As the Saint stepped outside, he was all too aware of the

perfect target he offered. A flicker of movement on his left caught his eye, and he sank to a crouch as he turned, perfectly balanced on his toes and ready to dive for cover at the first sign that the two men had decided to fight it out. The roofs of the adjoining houses were separated only by low brick walls from each of which rose a cluster of chimney pots.

Four houses away, the two terrorists were standing obviously uncertain of their next move. The Saint sprinted for the first dividing wall and cleared it in a flying leap that brought him safely behind the chimney stack of the house next door. The men spun around at the noise, but he was already hidden. Exposing only as much of his head as he needed to peer around the sheltering brickwork, he saw the smaller of the two point to the alley separating Little Claymore Street from the next road, and as his companion headed for a drainpipe, the smaller man ran on towards the end of the terrace.

The Saint flipped a mental coin that landed in favor of the man remaining on the roof. He swung over the next wall and then the one following that, darting from chimney to chimney as he went, without taking his eyes off the man he was pursuing, relying on his speed and sense of timing to ensure that every time the Arab turned he was already out of sight. He held the advantage of not having to worry where the chase led, while the other was constantly searching for a way of escape.

Gradually the gap narrowed until he was only a house away from his quarry.

The terrorist was kneeling at bay in the shadow of the next dividing wall no more than six yards away. The Saint ducked back behind his protective chimney stack, unable to make another move without inviting a bullet. He cursed himself for not bringing a gun, as he scanned the immediate area for anything that might serve as a weapon.

A ladder was propped against the attic roof, a pile of slates at its foot. The Saint slowly slid down until he was below the level of the wall and began to inch his way towards them. He drew level and gingerly reached out his hand. His fingers had touched and gripped the top slate before a shot rang out, kicking brick dust from the wall barely an inch from his thumb.

Simon grabbed up the slate and spun around. With only an instant in which to aim, he sent it hurtling through the air. It sliced into the gunman's wrist, sending the automatic clattering away across the roof.

Almost casually the Saint rose to his feet and brushed the dust from his hands.

"Why don't we see how brave you are without a gun or a bomb to rely on?" he drawled.

He placed one hand on top of the wall and vaulted over without taking his eyes off the Arab.

The terrorist stared at him like a snake hypnotised by a mongoose. He looked into two blue eyes that were as cold and passionless as an iceberg, and he felt his blood chill. He may have faced death many times, but always it had spurted from the end of a barrel, instant and acceptable. Clearly he had no stomach for the kind of manual punishment which he could happily dish out himself to a helpless girl, and which he could now see promised in the chiselled lines of this man's face.

He backed away as the Saint approached, frantically looking in every direction for an escape route. His heel caught against the frame of a skylight set in the roof. For a moment he swayed uncertainly and then he jumped, plunging down to land on the floor of the room below in a shower of glass and splintered wood.

Simon jumped forward and grasped an edge of the skylight frame that was free of jagged glass to swing himself through the opening, but the Arab was already out of the room and racing down the stairs. The noise had alarmed all the other residents of the house, and they crowded out of their rooms onto the stairs, blocking the Saint's path. Roughly he pushed them aside, but he already knew that the delays would prove long enough to allow the other's escape.

He reached the ground floor and sprinted out onto the pavement just in time to see the station wagon skid to a halt and the terrorist climb in.

The door had barely closed before the driver was taking the next corner on two wheels, and the Saint had no alternative but to stand and listen to the roaring engine fading into the distance.

4

The Saint accepted the setback philosophically. There would be a next time, and at least they had found the place they were looking for and knew how close their opponents were.

As he strolled back to the other house, he was glad to see that the crowds had dispersed as quickly as they had formed. No one seemed inclined to loiter at the scene of trouble, which meant that they were even less likely to summon the police.

Leila was bending over the girl, holding her chin in one hand and gently bathing the bruises with a wet cloth. She looked up hopefully as he entered, but he had to shake his head.

"They got away," he confessed.

"Damn," she said. "One was Masrouf, the other I think was his henchman Khaldun. At least we know that they too are still looking for Hakim."

She turned back to the girl, and he made a tour of the room, examining it in detail.

A single bed stood against one wall, a wardrobe and sofa against the other. The far end had been curtained off to hide an ancient gas stove. A single tap stuck out of the plaster above a chipped porcelain sink, beside which was the door leading to the roof. There was a musty damp smell that hung heavy on the air, and the boards beneath the threadbare carpet protested at every step.

The walls had been painted white and decorated with

brightly coloured prints and posters. Shelves of books had been fixed above the bed and sofa. Paisley drapes hung by the window. There was something rather pathetic about the personal touches that had been added. Instead of making the room more cheerful, they only served to underline its squalor.

A pile of school exercise books stood on the plain pine table in the centre of the room. Simon flicked through the top one, making a mental note of the name and address of the school.

"You teach mathematics?" he asked the girl they had rescued.

"Yes."

She tried to twist her head around to look at him, but Leila retained her grip although she had finished tending the injuries.

"There, that should take care of most of the swelling," Captain Zabin said crisply. "Now, what did you tell them?"

The girl was near to breaking point but managed to choke back her tears as she tried to meet Leila's piercing gaze.

"What could I tell them? I have never heard of this . . . this . . . you see, I don't even know his name."

Leila's voice was as hard as tungsten as she cut the girl short.

"Don't waste your tears on me."

"But I swear to you . . ."

"Nor your lies. Who is this?"

Leila thrust the photograph in front of her face. The girl grabbed at it but Leila drew it away.

"Where did you get that?" cried the girl.

"It was found after a Red Sabbath murder squad raided a village school," Leila replied coldly. "Thirteen people were slaughtered. Teachers like you, children like the ones you teach. Killed by that man and others like him."

"No! No, he wouldn't—"

The girl was sobbing, the tears running freely down her face, and the Saint realised that she was very close to hysteria.

"Who is he?" Leila pushed the girl's head back and held it so that she could not look away.

"He was no one. Rashid, a friend from Amman."

"That is Abdul Hakim. He is somewhere in London, and you know where. You will tell us."

The girl knocked Leila's arm aside and struggled to her feet. She swayed, and had to grip the back of a chair to save herself from falling.

"I don't care what you say about him! You have no right to question me like this. First those men, and now you. I am getting out of here!"

She crossed to the wardrobe, pulled out a battered suitcase, and began throwing her clothes into it.

Without moving, Leila said: "It doesn't interest you that your friend is a terrorist and a murderer?"

"I don't believe you."

"Listen," Leila said unemotionally, "this is a dangerous game you're playing. Your friend has killed a lot of innocent people. He'll kill a lot more unless he's stopped." The girl closed her case and made for the door, but Leila barred her way. "Think carefully. Talk to us, and we'll protect you. If we don't those men will track you down."

"They won't find me."

The Saint stepped forward and gently moved Leila aside. He stood in front of the girl and rested his hands lightly on her shoulders. His voice was soft and understanding.

"I'm afraid they will, Yasmina," he said. "My name is Simon Templar. If you change your mind or need help, call me at this number."

He took a card from his wallet and handed it to her. She stared at the name.

"The Saint!"

He smiled and held the door open for her.

"The same. Go away and think about it when you've calmed down."

He waited until the sound of her footsteps had died away before closing the door and turning to confront Leila. He could sense her fury, and he held up his hands in a gesture of peace.

"Before you sound off, think about it," he said. "She wasn't going to tell us now, and beating it out of her isn't in our line. There's been enough uproar around this neighbourhood for one day, and I have a nasty feeling that the lads in blue may arrive before too long—which is the last thing we want."

Leila relaxed fractionally and nodded.

"Yes, I suppose you are right," she admitted grudgingly. "But how did you know her name? She wouldn't tell me."

"It's written inside her books. Now there is something very important to do next."

"What? Follow her?"

"No. Eat. I haven't had a bite since breakfast, and that seems an eternity ago."

"But what about the girl?" Leila objected.

"I know where to find her if we need her. Now come on, or we'll have half the Metropolitan Police banging on the door, and I feel like something more substantial than porridge."

Despite her protests they drove back to the Saint's house, where Yakovitz informed them that no one had telephoned. Simon waved his hand in the general direction of the kitchen.

"The larder and the fridge are fully stocked, though I'm not sure how much of it is kosher," the Saint told him. "Or you can phone the local chop suey parlour and have them send something around. I'm taking your boss out to dinner." He winked at Leila. "Whether she likes it or not."

They dined in a small restaurant near Beauchamp Place. It was one of the Saint's favourite eating houses and had the added advantage of catering mainly to the nightclub trade, so that at that early hour of the evening it was almost deserted. They sat in a shadowed corner eating by the light of discreetly shaded candles. He remembered what his intention had been on leaving the plane from Nice, and was not dissatisfied with the way in which it had materialised.

The Saint attacked a rare entrecôte of noble proportions, while Leila picked at and toyed with her salmon. She initiated very little conversation, and he was content to carry most of the burden until the plates had been cleared away and they sat facing each other across coffee and cognac.

"Don't look so worried, Captain," he said at length. "We haven't made bad progress for just half a day's work. There's nothing more you can do tonight."

Leila stirred her coffee, looking down into the black liquid as if it possessed the same properties as a crystal ball.

"In our army we have a saying that to do nothing is to do something positively wrong. Don't you think perhaps we should be out looking for the girl Yasmina?"

The Saint sighed and sipped his brandy.

"You're a workotic, you know that?" Despite the mockery of his words his voice was sympathetic. "You're a one-track-minded object lesson of what goes wrong when you're brought up in a kibbutz."

He had expected a reaction, but nothing quite as heated as the one he evoked. Leila looked up, her face flushed, and she almost bit out her reply through clenched white teeth.

"How dare you!"

"I dare because I'm not afraid to face facts, even if you are," he said imperturbably. "You've been so long with the boys that you've forgotten they're boys and that you're a beautiful woman."

He watched the anger drain away from her face, but her voice was still sharp.

"I've forgotten nothing. What I look like . . . what I am—boy, girl, or mutant—is unimportant. I am . . ."

"I know, you're a soldier," he said. "And it's a shame that that's all there is to your life."

He waited for another angry outburst, but it never came.

Leila stared at the tablecloth for a long time, and when she raised her head and looked at him he saw that there were tears in her eyes.

"There is something else to it, Simon. Something more important than dining in a fine restaurant and a night in bed with you. There's my family and the memory of how they died. Mowed down with machine guns at Fiumicino airport. Father, mother, brother. I was eighteen."

Her voice had sunk to a whisper and was on the verge of breaking. He was angry with himself for having forced the declaration out of her when he had already half guessed her background that afternoon at the cathedral.

Simon reached across and gently took her hand.

"I'm sorry," he said. "Forgive me. But I had to know. If we're to work well together, it was important to know."

She drank her coffee and smiled back at him across the rim of the empty cup.

"It's all right. Perhaps I should have told you straight away. And you are right, there is nothing more we can do until the morning."

He called for the bill and paid it and did not speak again until they were back in the car.

"Actually, you misheard me," he said. "I didn't say there was nothing more *we* could do tonight. I said there was nothing more *you* could do. As far as I'm concerned, the night is still young."

"What do you mean?"

Simon smiled as he engaged the gears and turned the Hirondel towards Knightsbridge.

"Remember my friend who talks in code? Well, I have an appointment with him at ten of the clock, which is in precisely half an hour's time."

"And you don't intend to take me with you?"

"I didn't intend to," answered the Saint carefully. "I don't want to be specially noticed, and a gal with your looks is about as inconspicuous as a baked ham at a bar mitzvah."

He sensed that she was trying to be angry with him again but somehow couldn't quite take him seriously enough.

"You will take me with you," she commanded, with a delightful assumption of authority. "I refuse to be left behind."

The Saint laughed and placed an arm around her shoulders, drawing her slim body closer as he snaked the Hirondel through the traffic with one hand, which is not an example for other drivers to follow. He pushed his foot nearer the floor, and the big car surged forward towards the lights of Piccadilly.

He felt totally relaxed, but as alert and awake as if he had just slid from between the sheets after a good night's sleep.

"You just talked me into it," he said. "How could I disobey the orders of such a lovely officer? Of course you can come along. After all, I did promise to introduce you to some Londoners, and that's exactly what I'm going to do. I hope you're feeling fit, because we're likely to run into a spot of mayhem before morning."

5

The crowded streets and flashing neon of Leicester Square and the Strand were soon left behind, and with the assurance of a captain in familiar waters the Saint plotted a course through the sleeping backwaters of the City until the solid dignified shapes of the banks and insurance offices had disappeared behind them, to be replaced by a bewildering maze of dimly lit side roads lined by darkened shops and warehouses.

Leila watched the changing scenery without comment. She had hardly spoken for some time, and he could feel her tenseness returning.

"What's worrying you now?" he asked.

She straightened away from him and eyed his profile searchingly.

"It's just that there are so many questions we don't know the answers to," she said restively.

"Such as?"

"We had the picture and your knowledge of London to help us, but how did Masrouf and his men find Yasmina so quickly?"

Simon shrugged.

"Hakim and Masrouf were buddies in arms, remember? So it's quite possible that Hakim talked about her. Even if Masrouf didn't already have her address, the Arab community in London is a pretty small one, and he'd know where to go for information."

"Yes, I suppose so," she admitted. "But that only makes our task more difficult. We always seem to be one step behind."

"But Masrouf and Co. won't see it like that," explained the Saint patiently, "because they can't know how far we've got already. Masrouf didn't look surprised to see you, but he didn't know who I was, and it's my guess that that's worrying him. Right now, he's trying to find out who I am and what my part is—which promises well for future fun and games. Also it's a complication for him, and the longer we can distract him the more the odds swing in our favour."

"I hope you're right," she said, but she didn't sound convinced.

Simon smiled and gave her hand a reassuring squeeze before changing down through the gears.

"So do I," he said optimistically.

As the car slowed, he spun the wheel in a right turn that took them through an alley between two warehouses and out into a narrow lane running parallel to the major road they had just left. It consisted mainly of tiny shops and derelict houses separated occasionally by fenced-off patches of weed-covered rubble where buildings had been demolished and not replaced.

Simon berthed the car in a pool of darkness between two street lamps and cut the engine.

For a moment he sat and carefully took stock of their surroundings, satisfying himself that the lane was temporarily deserted, while he took a pair of horn-rimmed spectacles from the glove compartment and put them on. Then he got out and reached into the back seat for a mackintosh that might once have been a smart sandy beige but had long ago given up the struggle against the city grease and grime, and rammed a trilby of equally hard-worn lineage onto his head. The shabby raincoat covered up the elegant tailoring of Savile Row, and the thick frames of the glasses under the down-turned brim of the battered hat took the finely cut piratical edge off his features.

Leila had been watching the process of transformation with a puzzled frown.

"What is all that for?" she demanded.

"The hostelry I'm headed for is somewhat different from the one we just left," he explained, "and I don't want to be specially noticed. Or even recognised, except by the bloke I'm meeting," he added.

He went around to her side of the car, and she started to open her door, but he firmly closed it again.

"This is one place you can't come with me," he said. "It's a place where women are quite rudely made unwelcome. You'll just have to wait here. I'll only be about fifteen minutes. Wind up the window and keep the doors locked, and if anyone comes by, try to keep your pretty face hidden."

Resentfully, but bereft of any effective argument, she watched him slouch off down the lane at a brilliantly different gait from his normal athletic stride, and was forced to concede to herself, professionally, that his technique of subtle camouflage outpointed anything that could be done with elaborate props of the false-beard school.

The only signs of life in the lane were the lighted windows of the Carpenter's Arms. Simon pushed open the door of the public bar and entered like a regular, without looking around, ambling directly to the counter.

The interior was as unattractive as the red-tiled Victorian façade. The floor was covered with cracked linoleum and bordered with half a dozen heavy iron tables with marble tops the size of butchers' slabs, surrounded by hard wooden chairs. The wallpaper was so nicotine-stained that it was almost impossible to discern a pattern, and the decorations consisted chiefly of old photographs of coach outings and fixture lists for the darts team. The air was rank with the smell of stale beer and tobacco smoke. The handful of patrons looked up torpidly as the door opened, but seeing nothing remarkable about the newcomer, returned to their talk or their cribbage.

The Saint leant on the bar and ordered a half pint of best bitter. Only when the required measure had been dispensed and paid for did he appear to take an interest in his surroundings. The man he had come to meet was sitting alone at the far end of the room, and Simon allowed a couple of minutes to elapse before strolling across to join him.

Harry-the-Nose stood out against the seediness of his background like a carnival poster. He was a small, dapper figure who might even have been described as elegant if the check of his cut-price suit had been a trifle less dazzling, his tie a less conflicting array of stripes, or his socks a more harmonious hue. A synthetic diamond the size of a bottle cap sparkled from the centre of his tie, while a heavy gold signet ring weighted the little finger of the small meticulously manicured hand that held his whisky glass. His thinning hair was carefully brushed over the bald top of his head and kept in place by a glossy coating of pomade.

Members of what is popularly called the underworld have a tradition that is otherwise usually found only in barrack rooms and school playgrounds: a legal name is rarely considered sufficient by itself to identify its owner, and some graphic auxiliary is adopted or conferred. The most apparent reason for

Harry's particular cognomen was his outstanding facial feature, a nasal organ of such prominence that it cast the lower part of his face into permanent shadow. An even less flattering connotation of the sobriquet was his insatiable propensity for prying into other people's business and acquiring information which could be available to interested parties at a price.

Harry-the-Nose knew and accepted the title his peers had bestowed on him, but it was not wise to mention it in his presence. If he had ever heard of Cyrano de Bergerac he would have felt an immediate kinship, for his sensitivity also had caused him to fight duels in honour of the offending appendage, although instead of flashing rapiers at dawn he preferred a dark alley at midnight and a length of bicycle chain.

The Saint had collected Harry many years ago as part of his routine practice of making the acquaintance of anyone who might some day prove useful. Harry had demonstrated his worth on a number of occasions; and a bond had developed between them which, if it was not exactly welded by affection, was at least held together by mutual profitability.

Harry-the-Nose was valuable to the Saint because among his activities was the supply of tools for others to finish the job. When Mr. Public reads in his morning paper that a gang of bank robbers fled in an ambulance or that a man escaped from custody with the aid of a capsule of knockout gas, he marvels at the criminals' cunning but rarely stops to wonder how they obtain the necessary equipment. It was Harry's boast that he knew where to get anything from a driver's licence to a diving-bell, with no questions asked, and the Saint had no reason to doubt him. Harry's expertise was in constant demand, and there was rarely anything happening about which he did not know something.

The Saint sat down and took a pull at the liquid in his tankard, which tasted as if it might have been watered down with a mixture of liver salts and cold tea.

"Well, Harry," he prompted, what's the feeling?"

"Greasy," was the laconic reply. "Know what I mean?"

"Not exactly, but I can guess."

"These wogs are a funny lot," Harry opined. "Close knit, like, and dangerous. Talk their own lingo and don't mix. Nobody wants to deal with 'em. Unreliable."

"So what have you managed to find out?"

"Sammy Parton's doing the passport and visa. The order was placed by a twist, but it sounds like the one you're after."

The Saint nodded.

"It makes sense. Go on."

"That's about it, Mr. Templar. There was a bint last week who was asking around about getting a shooter. Somebody had told her where to go, but the lads didn't want to know. Too risky."

"And the other three I mentioned?"

"Ain't heard nothing about 'em. Sorry."

"That's okay, Harry," said the Saint. "Now listen, I've got another job for you . . ."

He outlined his commission, and then repeated the main points to make sure they had registered.

"Could be done," Harry said eventually, rubbing his salient feature reflectively. "But it'll cost you."

The Saint took a cigaret pack from his coat pocket and put it down beside his now empty tankard.

"There's the fifty quid I promised you, and another fifty on account. Don't worry, I'll see you through if the going gets rough."

He rose and walked away, leaving the cigaret package on the table for Harry-the-Nose to casually transfer to his own pocket before he reached the door.

6

Simon threw his hat and coat into the back of the car before sliding in behind the wheel and relaying the conversation to Leila. She was less than impressed.

"But how does that help us?"

He had already started the engine and turned the car around, heading back towards the main road.

"First," he informed her patiently, "we know the identity of the man who's forging the passport. Therefore he may be able to tell us where to find Hakim. Second, we know that he probably isn't armed. Third, Masrouf and his merry men have not been sniffing around, and so we have this particular field to ourselves. It's not sensational, but it's not bad for starters."

"And now we are going to this Parton man?"

"Correct. You catch on fast."

She scowled at his irony before turning her head away and concentrating on her own thoughts.

He was glad of the silence as it relieved him of the responsibility of projecting a confidence that he was far from feeling. He had obtained all the information he had hoped for from Harry, but he was all too conscious of how little it really was. There were so many loose ends that the slightest mishap could unravel the plan he was weaving.

Now he was zigzagging west and north towards Islington, drawing on a knowledge of London's unsystematic streets unmatched except by professional taxi drivers. Presently he braked in front of a grubby stationers' shop a couple of miles from the Carpenter's Arms as only a crow could have flown it, and was pleased to see that a light was burning in the flat above.

Leila looked at the shuttered shop window.

"This is Parton's?"

"Yes."

He opened the door and was about to climb out but she caught his arm.

"You are not leaving me behind again," she said.

For a moment the Saint hesitated. He knew she was a trained agent accustomed to violence and danger, yet he found it hard not to be protective. He realised that he was still hopelessly fettered to certain old-fashioned attitudes, and forced himself to remember that the times had changed and were never going to change back again. The mere fact that the girl beside him was a genuine army captain was a symptom that would have made Sir Galahad writhe in his armour.

"Very well," he said shortly. "But you'll have to do exactly as I say. And be careful. Parton keeps a tame gorilla on hand to discourage unfriendly callers, and he will consider us very unfriendly indeed."

He led the way past the shops and down a narrow passage between it and the next building. A seven-foot-high wall broken only by a door with no outside keyhole or handle enclosed what might have been the house's back garden and hid the ground floor of the building from view.

Bracing his back against the brickwork, he cupped his hands and motioned Leila to climb up, but she ignored his offer of help, took two steps back, and sprang for the top of the wall. He watched in admiration as she pulled herself up by her fingertips and in one flowing movement jumped down on the other side.

A few seconds later he landed beside her. Enough light came through the kitchen window curtains to show that they were in a neglected back yard in which amorphous stacks and mounds of undistinguished rubbish had prevailed over any other cultivation. The Saint stepped over to the kitchen door, and swore silently to himself as the testing pressure of his expert fingers indicated that the mortise lock was reinforced by a bolt which had been securely shot home. He moved along to the kitchen window, and after listening with an ear to the glass for any sound inside he carefully slid the thin blade of a penknife between the sashes until it grated against the catch. Pushing the blade further in he pressed sideways while his ears strained to pick up any warning sound that might mean that their intrusion had been spotted.

Slowly the catch began to move, and he applied more pressure until finally the blade met no resistance and he was able to press both hands against the glass and inch the window up. The rasping of the frame against its surround sounded as loud as a drum roll, and several times he stopped and waited to be sure that the noise had not disturbed the household.

He parted the curtains and listened again for the sound of anyone coming to investigate. Only when he was completely satisfied that his break-in had gone unheard, he swung himself over the sill and turned to help Leila to follow him. The instinctive courtesy was quite superfluous: almost disdainfully, she slid through the opening with hardly a touch on his proffered hand, and he grinned wryly at the remainder of her uncompromising competence.

Signalling her to let him stay in the lead, he moved to the door on the opposite side of the room and inched it open. A hall lit by an unshaded bulb stretched before him. Two doors led off from the left of the passage, while a staircase to the flat above took up most of the space on the right.

He beckoned Leila to follow and stepped into the corridor, treading warily along the edges of the bare boards to reduce the risk of their creaking. Leila followed his example and they had reached the foot of the stairs when the door of the back room was flung open.

The Saint spun around to find himself staring up into the face of one of the biggest men he had ever seen.

His lighthearted description of Parton's bodyguard as a gorilla suddenly seemed too accurate for comfort. The man filled the doorway, completely obscuring the interior of the room, and had to twist his body sideways to allow his shoulders through the opening. The Saint's sinewy seventy-four inches seemed insignificant compared to the man he faced. Simon guessed he was nearer six feet nine than eight, and on the heavier side of three hundred pounds.

But he did not spare the time to enquire if his estimate was correct. When it came to giving away that kind of weight and reach, Simon Templar's interpretation of sportsmanship and the Queensberry Rules was uninhibitedly elastic. Without an instant's hesitation, his foot streaked upwards and buried itself in the other's midriff.

The man grunted and sagged, his arms folded across his stomach, and as his head bowed forward the Saint moved in to hit him exactly as if he had been a punching bag with a lightning succession of blows—a left to one side of the jaw, a right to the other, and an uppercut to the chin to complete the symmetry.

Demonstrating the verity of the old adage that the bigger they are the harder they fall, the colossus stiffened and fell forward, with a kind of aggrieved expression on his face, hitting the floor with a force that seemed to shake the whole house.

Slowly the Saint came down off his toes, in no doubt that it would be many minutes before his opponent returned to an awareness of the world. He stepped over the body and joined Leila on the stairs.

She leant close to his ear and whispered: "Very efficient."

"Thank you," he murmured modestly.

His voice was almost at its normal level, and as they climbed the stairs he made little further effort to mask the sound of their progress, which he felt reasonably sure would now be attributed to movement of the immobilized bodyguard.

Three doors led from the landing above the hall, and the clanking of machinery indicated the one they required.

Sammy Parton turned around as he heard the door open, and froze in startlement as the Saint and Leila entered. Simon switched off the small printing press that had been making the noise and snapped his fingers in front of the forger's face.

"Wake up, Sammy! Anybody would think you weren't pleased to see us."

Parton stepped back, still staring at his two uninvited guests. He was small and fat, with a pointed face and sparse grey hair that brought to mind an ageing, overfed rat.

" 'Ow did you get in 'ere?" he demanded stupidly.

"We came in through a window," answered the Saint, as if to any normal question. "Your pet gorilla thought we shouldn't disturb you, but we managed to persuade him not to interfere."

Parton finally made a partial recovery.

"Orl right, Templar," he growled. "Wot d'yer want?"

"So you do remember me," said the Saint happily. "How very nice. And after all this time, too. How long has it been, Sammy? Three years? Four?"

"Five. And I ain't likely to forget, am I?"

"I suppose not. But you did get remission?"

Parton drew a packet of cigarets from the pocket of his ink-stained overalls and lit one.

"So wot do yer want?" he repeated. "I'm clean this time."

Simon smiled as his gaze travelled around the dirty print room and even dirtier printer, but there was no cordiality in his eyes.

"I wouldn't mind a couple of tickets for the cup final next year," he replied. "But failing that, just the answer to a simple question."

"Then you've come to the wrong bloke."

"You can't say that till you've seen the question," argued the Saint. He turned to Leila. "Show him."

Leila held up the picture of Yasmina and Hakim, and the forger was too slow to hide the recognition in his eyes.

"So thanks for the answer," Simon remarked. "Now, where is it?"

"Where's what?"

The top drawer of the desk that Parton was standing next to was slightly open, and the little man's hand was slowly edging towards it. The Saint affected not to notice the movement as he pressed on with his interrogation.

"The passport that you are so artistically creating for the gent in the photo," he said.

"I dunno wot yer talkin' about," Parton insisted stubbornly. His fingers had reached the lip of the drawer. "You come in 'ere . . . break in 'ere . . ."

Parton stepped forward, putting his body between the drawer and the Saint. It was a perfectly natural move, and it was almost a pity to spoil the performance.

The Saint's hand landed squarely in Parton's chest, and as the little man staggered backwards, Simon's right foot kicked the drawer closed. Parton squealed as his fingers were trapped.

Simon eased the pressure sufficiently to allow the other to remove his hand but not to extract the gun he had been groping for. While Parton massaged his bruised fingers, the Saint retrieved the automatic, removed the magazine, ejected the cartridge in the firing chamber, and tossed the weapon into a wastepaper basket.

"Any more tricks like that, Sammy," he warned, "and I shall get upset. Now, where's the passport? Or do I have to tear this rat hole apart and you with it?"

The forger's eyes burned with hate, but there was a lift of triumph in his voice.

"Go ahead," he jeered. "Enjoy yourself. It won't do you a bit of good. It ain't under this roof."

"I see," Simon deduced. "So when a job's finished, you put it in a safe place where the client can't come and pick it up with a gun instead of cash."

Parton puffed sullenly at his cigaret without replying.

"All right," said the Saint. "The passport's ready. You've said as much. Now I want the place and date of delivery."

"Templar, some day you'll get it through your head that I don't grass on customers."

Leila stepped forward, and Parton turned to give her his full attention for the first time.

"Suppose I buy this man's passport from you for double what he would pay?" she asked.

Parton shook his head as if he was genuinely sorry to disappoint her.

"Lady, I do that and I'm a goner. This ain't the usual run of client."

The Saint's voice came low and hard: "Yes, he's a killer. But then you knew that, didn't you?"

The little fat man was sweating, torn between fears of what the Saint might do if he refused to answer and what others would certainly do if he did.

"Templar, put yourself in my place. A bloke such as you describe orders a passport. I don't talk about it. If anything goes wrong at the market tomorrow when I make the drop, I'll be gettin' measured for a coffin."

"Which market, Sammy?" Simon pounced on the word remorselessly.

Parton wiped the sweat from his forehead and lit a new cigaret from the butt of the old one.

"Market? Did I say market? Just leave me alone, will you? Clear off and leave me alone!"

The Saint's sensitive ears picked up sounds of movement in the hall below that could only have come from one source. Parton obviously heard them too, and his confidence began to return.

"You'd better get out of here, Templar, while yer still can," he threatened.

The Saint smiled, and his hand reached across and patted the other's cheek in a mockery of affection.

"Thanks for the help, Sammy," he responded. "We'll see you around."

He turned towards the door, but Leila stood in the way without moving.

"Surely," she protested. "You're not . . ."

Simon shook his head.

"No, I'm not. Staying for Goliath, that is. Not until we can book Wembley Stadium and sell tickets. But here and now, there's nothing more in it for us. Believe me."

He took her by the arm and led her out of the room and down the stairs. The bodyguard was sitting with his back against a wall, gingerly feeling his jaw and shaking his head muzzily. He glared up at them vengefully, but was still in no condition to make any move to stop them as the Saint found the door to the shop, took Leila through it, unlocked the front door, and led them out into the street.

Leila sat in prickly silence as he headed the car back towards the West End. He could feel the anger building up inside her, and tried to dampen the fuse.

"Think it through a bit further before you blow your top, darling," he said quietly. "The passport isn't there, and short of tying up Goliath and sticking pins under Sammy's fingernails we couldn't have found out how it's to be delivered. But if we could have made Sammy tell us, the delivery would have been off. As it is, we know he'll be meeting Hakim tomorrow, and Hakim is the guy we really want. We'll just have to make sure that we're there when they get together."

"You are the guide," she retorted coldly. "I am forced to count on you to make certain that we are there."

The suspicion remained in her voice, and confirmed him in a mildly malicious decision not to dispel it by going into details.

"Don't worry," he said cheerfully. "I shall."

They completed the drive without speaking again. The Saint was thinking about other things. He was quite satisfied with what they had achieved that night, and was perfectly content to let the morrow wait for itself. Hakim, Masrouf, and even Leila were far from uppermost in his thoughts when he turned the Hirondel into the mews.

The cul-de-sac was lit only by a solitary lamp at the far end, and he was into it before he saw the station wagon outside his house, facing towards him. Even so, its identity took a second to register, and by then it was too late.

He stamped on the brake as something shattered the glass of his sitting room window. The station wagon leapt forward and came swerving past them just as a terrific explosion blew out the rest of the front ground-floor windows.

7

As the station wagon careered past them he had barely a glimpse of two swarthy faces in it—Khaldun, probably, in the driver's seat, his head stretched forward over the wheel, while the man beside him, looking back over his shoulder at the destruction he had caused, could have been Masrouf.

Leila Zabin moved with startling speed, reacting to the situation with reflexes sharpened by intensive training. While the Hirondel was still rocking to a standstill, her hand dived into her purse and a small automatic was in her grasp by the time it righted itself. Before the Saint could stop her, she was out of the car and taking two-handed aim. She fired as soon as her outstretched arms reached the level of her shoulders, but could only crack off two hasty rounds as the station wagon turned the corner.

The Saint threw himself out of the car and grabbed her around the waist as she began to sprint for the opening.

"Don't be a fool," he snapped. "You'll never catch them now."

She shook him off but made no move to continue her pursuit. Slowly she lowered the gun.

"For God's sake put that thing away," he said.

One or two windows overlooking the mews were opening, and Leila saw the sense of his advice. She pushed the automatic into the waistband of her skirt, where her coat would cover it. Nevertheless, whether from timidity or the apathy of the big city, there was as yet no rush of inquisitive neighbours to gawp at whatever the big bang might have produced to gawp at.

Simon realised that as loud as the detonation had seemed to him, because he had been so close and seen its immediate effect, anyone a little farther away might have dismissed it, perhaps wishfully, as merely an especially loud backfire or a major collision of vehicles. But in retrospect he was now fairly sure that he could tell what it had been: an ordinary hand grenade.

By that time he was opening the door of the house, with Leila close behind him.

The bomb had gone off near the middle of the room, fortunately in an area where surrounding armchairs and a couch had absorbed the brunt of its havoc. This had not entirely saved the walls and ceiling from being pockmarked by fragments of flying metal, the shattering of some ornaments and picture frames, and the gouging in the carpet of a shallow, smouldering crater which no shampooing and weaving service was ever going to restore. All the same, the blast had not been severe enough to cause any radical structural damage.

The Saint stood completely still as he surveyed the debris through the dust and smoke that lingered in the air. There was a strange, unnatural calm about him that was somehow more frightening than a torrent of threats against those responsible could ever have been. As far as he was concerned, there could be no more standing on the sidelines. The conflict of tribes and ideologies about which he had previously felt only a biased neutrality was suddenly of secondary importance. Now his own home had been violated. Furniture could be quickly replaced, and surfaces patched up, but the savage invasion of his most private territory had created a personal debt that could only be personally repaid.

There was also another person to think of--such a recent and secondary addition to his concerns that the Saint had momentarily forgotten him.

"Yakovitz!" Leila's tensely anxious voice was his reminder.

"Yakovitz?" Simon echoed her mechanically.

There was certainly no trace of her subordinate in the shattered living room, which could have been a hopeful sign. And then a low moan, hardly above a whimper, came from the kitchen.

Yakovitz was lying face down on the kitchen floor in a litter of broken crockery and overturned utensils. As the Saint knelt down and felt for his pulse, he stirred and opened his eyes. He shook his head slowly and pulled himself up until he was half sitting, half kneeling.

"Take it easy," said the Saint. "Keep still."

His fingers gently probed the other's body, but Yakovitz didn't flinch. Satisfied that there was no serious injury, he soaked a towel and tried to wipe away the dust and stains from the man's face, but Yakovitz took it away and did it himself.

"I am all right," he growled. "I was only knocked-out."

Apparently he had been brewing himself some coffee when the grenade smashed through the window, and enough of the blast had come through the open doorway to throw him across the kitchen, and he had hit his head as he fell. Aside from one or two scratches, he had suffered nothing worse than a mild concussion.

Simon helped him back to the living room and into one of the still serviceable armchairs.

"He's a lucky lad, is your Yakovitz," he told Leila. "A few minutes earlier or later, and we'd probably have been scraping bits of him off the walls."

"Lucky," Yakovitz said stoically, "I have a thick head."

Most of the bottles and glasses on the hospitality table were in smithereens, but the Saint found a bottle of cognac and a glass that had miraculously survived, and poured Yakovitz a hefty tot.

"While that's making your head thinner," he said, "I'd better do something about making our drama less public."

Outside the front windows there were brightly painted shutters hinged to the wall, ostensibly to give the house a pleasantly rustic air, but they were also functional. Simon had just closed and secured them when a blue-uniformed figure loomed up at his shoulder.

"Would this be where that explosion was?" enquired the Law.

"Oh, did you hear it, or did somebody phone in?" countered the Saint ingenuously, giving himself a moment in which to think.

"Must've been here," returned the police sergeant, thoughtfully crunching some of the telltale shards of glass on the cobblestones under his feet.

He was clearly nearing retirement age, and the expression on his plump face as he tried ineffectually to peep through the shutter louvres suggested that he was more accustomed to feeling collars than coping with terrorists.

"Sounded quite like a bomb, it did," he mentioned stolidly.

"I know," said the Saint. "The theory is that I, being me, have a great many enemies who wish to enrol me in the celestial choir, and this was obviously the work of one of them. Sorry to disappoint you, but it was nothing so sensational. We must have had a small leak in the gas oven. A friend of mine who doesn't have such a good sniffer went into the kitchen and struck a match, and it went off with a bang. Fortunately, he wasn't hurt. Just a few broken dishes, and all this glass blown out."

"I see," said the sergeant, as if he rather regretted it. "But since there'll have to be a report, now, would you mind coming around to the station and making a statement?"

"If I can be any help to the Metropolitan Police," said the

Saint resignedly, "nothing is too much trouble. Just let me make my excuses to my guests."

It was almost two hours before he eventually arrived home again, to find Leila curled up on the settee asleep. Her slender figure was wrapped in his own silk dressing-gown, and she looked so innocent and vulnerable that he found it hard to credit that a little earlier she had been wielding a pistol with the cold professionalism of a seasoned commando.

She awoke with a start at the clink of glass on glass.

"Simon! Well? What happened?"

He settled on the arm of the chair opposite and sipped his brandy before replying.

"I believe the official phrase is 'helping the police with their enquiries.' I have been going through the charade of dictating a statement and waiting for it to be typed by some one-fingered truncheon wielder who was as meticulous as if he'd been bidding for a Nobel Prize. I have been signing same and answering a hundred and one questions arising therefrom, all designed to trap me into admitting some kind of guilt or of knowing some guilty person. Of course, I stuck by my gas-leak story, since you and Garvi want to keep the cops out of it." He took another sip. "How's Yakovitz?"

"All right. But I ordered him to bed."

Simon glanced around the room again.

"While you did the housework," he said. "Thanks for cleaning up the mess, Leila."

"It was the least I could do. Your beautiful home, wrecked, because of us . . ."

She stood in front of him, and there was a mistiness in her eyes that he had not expected.

"Simon, I'm sorry about how I have spoken to you sometimes." Her voice trembled slightly. "But when my work here is finished—"

He drew her close and smothered the rest of her words with

a kiss. When their lips finally parted she made no move to leave his embrace.

"When your work here is finished, we'll have time to talk of many things," he said.

She was about to speak again, but he placed a finger against her lips.

"But not now," he said. "And the business talk will keep till breakfast. Go on up to bed, and I'll doss down here."

Despite the strain of the long night, the Saint was still the first to rise. He had long ago cultivated the ability to keep firing with only a minimum of sleep. He had slumbered peacefully and awakened refreshed at the reveille of his own mental alarm clock, to shower and change his clothes before he roused the others.

Leila came down to the invigorating aroma of percolating coffee and sizzling bacon. Yakovitz followed more slowly, but his step was steady and his eyes clear.

"I hope my heathen habits won't spoil your appetites," Simon apologised as he seated them. "But you can still eat the eggs."

Leila had changed back to the fawn tailored suit she had worn when they met, and its faintly military style helped her return to outward impersonality.

"I telephoned Colonel Garvi and told him everything that has happened," she stated, as if making a formal report.

"And has he any jolly new ideas?" asked the Saint.

Leila nodded.

"Yes. As soon as we have Hakim we are to take him to another base, a house the embassy owns near Epping. I have written down the address."

"Why?"

She looked surprised at the question.

"For interrogation," she answered. "We can't ask you to let us keep him here, and the embassy is not suitable."

The Saint shrugged.

"What you do with him is your affair," he said callously. "My job finishes when we catch him. After that, I'm going to have a few scalps of my own to collect."

"Simon, how do you think Masrouf knew where to find us?"

The Saint buttered another slice of toast.

"That's been puzzling me too. The only answer I can think of is that he did an about-turn after we scared him off yesterday, and followed us when we left the flat. I'm afraid it didn't occur to me that he might have got back on our tail so quickly. For which I've been taught a damn good lesson."

"Colonel Garvi said I should tell you that of course we shall pay for the damage."

"I'm sure you will," said the Saint. "But you can't write a cheque for everything I'm holding against the Red Sabbath. Never mind that for now. We've got a busy day ahead."

"What is your plan?" Leila asked.

"We keep close to Yasmina. My guess is that it'll be her job to make the contact with Parton, but that Hakim won't be very far away. So eat up, or we'll be late for school."

The Hirondel had survived the explosion with no more serious damage than a few scratches in the paintwork caused by flying glass. They drove east, following a similar route to the one they had taken the night before. They passed through Whitechapel into Stepney and stopped at last opposite the gates of a modern primary school. The only other vehicles in the road were a yellow van parked a few yards behind a small coach.

Yasmina stood by the gates shepherding children into the coach. In the yellow van, a man sat low in the driving seat with his face buried in the racing pages of a morning newspaper.

The Saint turned to Leila.

"Do you know the phone number of that house at Epping?"

She told him, and he scribbled a few words on a visiting card which he handed to Yakovitz.

"Walk over the road," he said, "and drop this through the driver's window of that van as you pass. Then come back."

Yakovitz obeyed without asking for a reason or even reading the card.

As they watched the maneuver being completed, Leila asked: "Who is in that van?"

"That is Harry-the-Nose," said the Saint. "Last night I told him to follow Yasmina and report back everything she did, but that was before I found out that the drop was to be today. Still, there's no reason why he can't follow her too as a sort of double insurance, in case we get separated for any reason. I gave him the phone number in Epping in case I have to go there with you."

Yakovitz climbed back into the car as the last of the children boarded the coach. As it moved off, the Saint slid smoothly in behind it, keeping an eye on the rear view mirror to be certain that the yellow van had joined the convoy.

They headed for the Commercial Road and back towards the City, edging their way slowly through the crawling traffic. They skirted the Tower and swung left over London Bridge, turning sharply across to the right as soon as the south bank of the river was reached. As the coach pulled into the kerb beside Southwark Cathedral, the Saint drove on and stopped out of sight around the next corner.

The Borough Market is a mini Covent Garden standing beside Southwark Cathedral in the shadow of London Bridge. Traders conduct their business from open pitches beneath a glass roof supported by thick iron pillars. It is situated in the centre of two access roads leading from the main thoroughfare of Southwark Street. Between the market and the riverside sprawls a web of narrow lanes that twist between towering blocks of warehouses and depositories. The air is thick with the smell of rotting fruit and the distinctive ozone of the Thames. From dawn until midday it is a bedlam of noise and hurrying people.

The Saint looked up at the plaque fixed to the wall on the opposite side of the lane where he had parked, and grinned.

"Clink Street. I can think of quite a few people who think I should have stopped here years ago."

Leila frowned.

"I do not understand."

"I'll explain some other time," he said hastily.

"Yakovitz, you find a spot on the stairs leading from the front of the cathedral to the bridge. From there you should get a clear view of everything that moves. Leila, you take the viaduct arches so that you can watch the entrance to the cathedral without too much risk of Yasmina spotting you."

"And you?"

"I'll go through the market and try and find Parton. Our best chance lies in jumping Hakim when he shows to collect the passport. Yakovitz, you go now. Leila, you follow in a minute. We'll be too obvious if we keep together. Okay?"

They both nodded, and Yakovitz got out of the car. The events of the night had combined to place the Saint in charge of the operation, and neither of the others thought to question his command.

Yakovitz strolled back into the road that separated the market from the cathedral, and turned in through the wrought-iron gates to cross the precinct immediately in front of the church. Except for Yasmina and her charges standing outside the main doors waiting for their guide, and a couple of tramps asleep on the benches, the area was deserted.

Simon stood at the top of the bridge steps and watched Leila walk past, using the coach to screen her from Yasmina. Behind the coach, Harry was lounging in his van, resuming his studies of the racing columns, apparently oblivious of everything else.

The Saint strode quickly through the back lanes, memorising every twist and turn until he reached the rear entrance to the market.

Two main aisles divide the market into quarters, which are then split into irregular sections by the tall wire pens from which the traders sell. Simon stopped at the junction of the two aisles; from there he had a clear view of the entrance roads on either side. The coach stood opposite the end of the east aisle.

The driver left his seat and climbed down to the pavement. For a while he stood looking across at Yasmina and the children before turning towards the market. As he did so he pushed his peaked cap to the back of his head, and the Saint found himself staring at the face of Abdul Hakim.

8

Hakim stood beside the coach glancing nervously each way before crossing the road and entering the market. He looked older than in the photograph. The cheeks were more hollow and the forehead more lined. The mass of curly hair was uncombed and he had not shaved for a couple of days. He wore a zipper jacket of black leather and tight black corduroy trousers. He moved with the furtive grace of an outcast cat poised to fight or run at any instant, but his eyes had the shifty look of the hunted rather than the hunter.

Simon stepped back into a narrow passage between some piled-up crates and waited as Hakim walked slowly down the main aisle towards him. All around him the porters and traders continued with their noisy everyday business; a few of them looking curiously at the Saint as they passed. He took a notebook from his pocket and pretended to count the boxes and tick them off on an imaginary list while he listened to the sound of Hakim's footsteps coming nearer.

He was somewhat surprised by the ease with which the trap was preparing to be sprung. Simply to have to wait until Hakim walked into his arms seemed almost an anticlimax after the events of the preceding twenty-four hours, but he had no wish to quarrel with the Fates for smoothing his path.

The clamour of the market, which had seemed almost deafening at first, had now adjusted itself in his hearing into a permanent background which he could screen out of his consciousness while he followed Hakim's wary progress along the aisle. Quite apart from that generalised noise, his ears recorded a sound of footsteps approaching from behind him, but his brain was a split-second slow in reacting to them as a danger signal.

He had only half turned when the massive arms of Parton's bodyguard closed around his chest in a suffocating bear hug. In the same moment he felt himself lifted clear of the ground and hurled through the air as if he weighed no more than a child's doll.

He had a fleeting glimpse of the forger running past him towards Hakim, before he crashed backwards into a pile of crates that collapsed with the impact and sent him sprawling against the concrete floor. The air was forced from his lungs in one long gasp, and a kaleidoscope of flashing lights danced before his eyes as his head touched the ground.

He felt every bone in his back and shoulders jar with the impact, and only the responses of a veteran fighter saved him as the giant waded in for the kill. Instinctively he rolled to one side and the kick that should have sent him to join all the historic saints actually parted the top of his hair.

As his vision cleared, he saw the giant poising himself to resume the attack. The sheer bulk of the man made him ponderously slow, but the Saint was all too aware that just one blow squarely landed from those huge fists could prelude the end of the contest.

With one hand flat on the ground, he pushed himself up into a squat and dived sideways at the gorilla's legs. His arm folded under the man's knees as his shoulder cannoned into his thighs. The giant swayed for a moment as he tried to maintain his balance, but the Saint's momentum was too great and he toppled backwards to land flat against the concrete with his arms flailing the air as he tried clumsily to break the force of his fall.

The Saint was on his feet again in an instant. There was no

time for the niceties of the brawl that should have followed. Already he could see Hakim and Parton concluding their transaction and in a few seconds the Arab would be beyond his reach.

Parton stared blankly at the Saint as if he could hardly believe that he was still a threat. The forger's face was disfigured by a strip of sticking plaster that ran from the corner of his right eye to the side of his mouth. Beneath it the skin was puffed and black. The sight raised a large question mark in the Saint's mind, but he had no spare time just then to spend on speculating about that interesting embellishment.

He started to run past the fallen giant, but the man flung out a wild arm that half tripped him. As he reached out for anything to save him from falling, his hand fastened on the top of a tier of packing cases. As he recovered his balance he yanked the top crate free. The bodyguard stared up in horror as the heavy wooden box plummeted down with the Saint augmenting the force of gravity with his own strength, but there was nothing he could do to break its fall. His whole frame went rigid as it smashed on his head, and his participation in the further proceedings discontinued.

Without waiting to administer first aid, Simon hurdled the obstacle and raced towards the main aisle, roughly shoving aside the gaping spectators who had been attracted to the commotion.

Hakim had turned and fled as soon as he saw the Saint rise, and Parton was not much slower off the mark in sprinting in an opposite direction. Simon ignored the forger and followed Hakim. The terrorist ran back into the road beside the coach. For a moment he wavered, unsure of his next move, and the Saint rapidly closed the gap between them.

He could see Yakovitz rushing across the cathedral precincts while Leila moved in from the other end of the street. Yasmina had deserted her children and was running towards her lover, frantically waving her arms and shouting a warning in some language the Saint did not understand.

Hemmed in on three sides, there was only one possible escape route left open and Hakim took it. He turned and tore down the road leading to the river front behind the cathedral.

Simon was about to follow when he heard a shot, and he had dodged for the cover of a parked lorry before he realised that he was not the target. The bullet shattered the glass of a street lamp as Hakim ran beneath it.

The Saint spun around as the blue station wagon screeched to a halt and Masrouf, Khaldun, and the man he had seen outside Yasmina's flat the previous afternoon, jumped out. It was clear that they had eyes only for Hakim and appeared unaware of either Leila or Yakovitz closing in behind. All three men carried revolvers, and Yakovitz and Leila had also brought their guns into the open.

When the lamp glass shattered, Hakim increased his speed, bending low and swaying from the hips as he ran, but the three terrorists did not fire again. Simon scooted around the lorry and came out on the other side as Hakim disappeared around the corner to where the Hirondel was parked. Masrouf and Khaldun ran after him, leaving their companion to bring up the rear and cover them.

The Saint sprinted back into the market, dodging between the wire cages and following a diagonal route that brought him out into a road running at right angles to the one Hakim had taken. The sound of more shots reached him, but he had no way of knowing who was firing at whom.

He stopped for a moment to get his bearings before crossing the road and entering a lane sloping off to the right. After about fifty yards it opened into a large cobbled square that served as a parking and unloading area for the warehouses that lined it on every side. The only other exit was an alley in the far corner, and the Saint ran towards it.

He was halfway across the square when Hakim emerged from the alley. He stopped as soon as he saw the Saint, and looked desperately in every direction. The sound of shouts and running feet echoed from the passage behind him. Unable to go either forward or back, he jumped onto the loading bay of the nearest warehouse and plunged blindly into the shadowy interior.

The Saint leapt after him and had barely gained the shelter of the platform before Masrouf and Khaldun burst into the square. They stopped just outside the mouth of the alley, uncertain of their next move, but the decision was made for them when a bullet clipped the brickwork above their heads. Masrouf turned and fired a reply without taking aim, and the two men dashed across the cobbles to disappear down the lane from which the Saint had emerged a few seconds before.

Inside the warehouse, Simon turned from watching Yakovitz chase the fleeing Arabs and looked for Hakim.

The loading bay led into a cavernous storeroom stacked almost to the ceiling with wooden crates. At the far end a wide flight of iron steps led up to a gantry that circled the walls. There was no sign of Hakim. The Saint moved soundlessly in a narrow passage between the crates, every nerve taut, his eyes and ears straining to catch any sight or sound that might reveal Hakim's hiding place. He reached the stairs and slowly began to climb, intending to use the gantry to gain a bird's-eye view of the storeroom below.

As he reached the first landing the Arab broke cover and ran back towards the loading bay. There was an iron crowbar clutched in his hand, and two workmen who had just climbed in, rapidly backed away as he approached.

Simon cursed the luck with which he had been eluded, and returned to the floor in two leaps.

Hakim must have been in fair condition and had made good use of his few minutes' rest in the warehouse to recover his breath. He set a fast pace across the square, and doubled back down the alley heading for the river.

The Saint settled his stride and prepared for a lengthy pursuit, content to gradually whittle down the other's lead and sap his strength. By the time Hakim reached the wider road that separates the warehouses from the wharves Simon was only about thirty yards behind.

The road ran straight until it passed under the arches of Southwark Bridge a quarter of a mile farther on. On the right, a low wall divided the road from the landing stages that serve the barges bringing cargo from the large freighters in the Pool beneath the Tower to the warehouses upriver from London Bridge. On the left was an unbroken line of buildings with not even an alley between them to provide an alternative bolthole.

The river sparkled in the sunlight, distorting the reflection of the trains pulling slowly into Cannon Street Station. In mid-stream a tug was nursing a flotilla of heavily laden barges. A couple of pleasure boats crammed with camera-clicking tourists chugged sluggishly beneath the arches of London Bridge. The passengers peered and pointed as they listened to the guide's running commentary on the sights to be seen along the south bank, trying to pinpoint the site of Shakespeare's Globe Theatre while completely unaware of the contemporary drama that was being played under their eyes.

The Saint began to sense an uncertainty in Hakim's movements. The terrorist's pace was slowing and his steps faltered as he frantically looked in every direction for a way of escape. Inexorably Simon increased the pressure. Hakim glanced back over his shoulder, and the sight of the Saint so close on his heels made him dredge up the last of his reserves of stamina. He attempted one final spurt, but the strength had left his legs and after a few yards he stumbled and almost fell.

The Saint realised that the chase was over. What for him had been a fairly healthy workout appeared to have reduced Hakim to the semblance of a wet Arabian nightshirt. He reeled against the low wall between the road and the line of jetties, desperately sucking in air and wiping the sweat from his forehead and eyes.

Simon Templar slackened his stride to a walk as Hakim

stayed and slumped against the wall, and came up to stand behind him.

"Had enough?" he asked mockingly. "There's no where to run, Hakim. Nowhere else to hide."

Hakim did not answer. His back was turned to the Saint and his hand cradled in the crook of his right elbow, the crowbar he had picked up somewhere in the warehouse still slackly held in the same hand. The Saint reached out a hand towards his shoulder and in the same instant Hakim spun round, the crowbar slicing through the air in a murderous arc.

9

Only the Saint's whiplash reflexes saved him from a fractured skull. He recoiled instinctively, stepping backwards and arching his body sideways.

The speed and ferocity of Hakim's attack was too great for his own equilibrium, and he stumbled forward. The Saint straightened, perfectly poised on the balls of his feet and smiled into the Arab's face.

"Naughty, naughty," he taunted reprovingly and sent a straight left flicking into the other's nose.

The terrorist winced at the pain as he quickly backed out of reach of a follow-up punch, and wiped away the trickle of blood with the back of his hand. He glared at the Saint with fear and hatred in his dark eyes. His lips drew tight against his teeth as he sprang forward, again scything the air with the crowbar.

It was a contest between the boxer and the barroom bully, only in slightly different terms, and although he never doubted the inevitable outcome, the Saint did not underestimate the desperation of his cornered opponent. He simply felt entitled to a little sporting exercise in return for the trouble he had been given.

Simon Templar danced. With his arms hanging loosely at his sides, he relied on sheer speed and agility to escape the murderous assault Hakim mounted. He bobbed and weaved and rode the blows measuring distance to the micro-fraction of an inch. And all the time he smiled impudently at his assailant; and the more he smiled, the more angry the Arab became and the more erratic his attacks.

The commotion had attracted the inevitable crowd that always seems to appear as if from the air when seconds before there was no one in sight. They gathered at a safe distance, gaping at the spectacle but not eager to get involved.

It could have been great fun for all, but it had to be cut short. The Saint quickly moved in and proceeded with some relish to take the terrorist apart with a few bruising body punches that ended Hakim's wild swings and drove the Arab cowering back against the cold stone of the river wall. The Saint felt no pity: Hakim was more than just one man, one murderer. He symbolised his breed; so brave when faced with helpless hostages, the young and old and weak, with the job of planting a bomb to go off when he was well away, but with no stomach for face-to-face conflict on equal terms.

At that moment the Saint was aware of the unmistakeable throaty growl of the Hirondel. It stopped beside them with a scream of protesting rubber and he turned to see Yakovitz climb out of the driver's seat.

"Here's your excess baggage," he called out, and while Yakovitz opened the rear door he sent a final left hook jolting into the point of Hakim's chin.

As the Arab slid earthwards, the Saint caught him by the collar and the seat of the pants to throw him headfirst into the car. Yakovitz jumped in on top of him, and the Saint slid in behind the wheel and took the big car roaring away, scattering the spectators from its path.

The entire spontaneous pickup was accomplished as neatly as if they had rehearsed it, and the Saint chortled with delight.

"Right on cue! I was beginning to wonder what I was going to do with him. What happened back there?" he asked as he forced a way through the traffic clogging Southwark Bridge.

Yakovitz answered slowly as if embarrassed to admit his failure.

"Captain Zabin stayed to deal with the third man while I chased Masrouf and Khaldun. They split up, and I followed Masrouf, but I lost him in the alleys, so I went back to help her. By the time I got to the market again there was no sign of her, but two policemen were arriving. I went back to your car and came looking for you."

"And you have no idea what happened to Leila?" Simon asked, frowning.

Yakovitz shook his head.

"No. As I said, when I got back after losing Masrouf there was no sign of her. She may have slipped away when the police came, or she could have followed the other man somewhere. I did not see your friend Harry, either."

"That's some consolation, anyway," Simon remarked. "Harry isn't the sort of person who'd join in, but neither is he the type who cuts and runs when the going looks rough. I hired him to follow and watch, and that's probably just what he did, he'll make contact later. He should be able to tell us where Leila went."

"Captain Zabin is one of our most experienced operatives," said Yakovitz stiffly. "I am sure she will be all right."

"So am I," Simon agreed.

He could tell that Yakovitz's assumption of his superior's safety was based more on loyalty than logic, and he also was somewhat less confident than he cared to show.

He drove through the City and headed east until they reached the main Newmarket road. After a few miles the long lines of houses and shops began to peter out and they entered the brown and green woodland of Epping Forest.

"Do you know how to find the house that Captain Zabin was talking about?" he asked presently.

"If you find the Bell Post House first, I can direct you."

The Saint had once stopped at the hotel at Bell Common, and with that as an easy landmark, he could relax for a while into almost automatic driving. There were no interruptions from Hakim, but from certain movements that he occasionally glimpsed in the rear-view mirror, he had the impression that Yakovitz was taking such steps as were necessary, from time to time, to ensure that the terrorist remained in the comatose state to which the Saint's punishment had reduced him.

The woods gradually gave way to fields of wheat and corn that stretched away into the distance with only an occasional tree or barn breaking the shallow contours of the landscape. As they moved farther from the forest and deeper into the farmlands it was almost impossible to believe that they were only an hour from the centre of London.

Yakovitz seemed disinclined for idle conversation, and the Saint used the silence to assess the situation. Whichever way he looked at it, he realised that the game was still far from over. They had succeeded in grabbing Hakim, and therefore whatever happened next, they held the trump card. They had the added advantage that Masrouf and company could have no idea where they were taking Hakim. Leila was the only problem; and the more Simon considered her disappearance, the more uncertain he became that his side would be able to completely dictate the next move.

From the Bell Post House, he followed Yakovitz's directions until they swung onto a rutted, unpaved road that wound through a thin belt of trees to peter out before a pair of tall iron gates that were the only break in a high redbrick wall. Beyond the gates, a gravel drive swept in a wide arc for some three hundred yards until it reached an elegant white stone house of the sort that real estate agents are moved to call a luxurious country residence.

As soon as the Hirondel stopped at the gates, two men emerged from the shelter of the wall. Both carried shotguns, and while one levelled his weapon at the occupants of the car, the other opened one gate and walked over to the driver's side of the car. He scrutinized the pass that Yakovitz extended and finally nodded to his companion, who lowered his gun and opened the other gate. The man who had come out spoke briefly into a two-way radio that he took from his breast pocket and waved them through.

Hakim was beginning to come around once again by the time they pulled up at the portico but he offered no resistance when Yakovitz dragged him roughly from the car and half carried, half dragged him up the wide steps.

Inside, the air was stale and heavy with the tang of mothballs and sickly smell of fresh paint. The furniture was hidden under white dust sheets, and there were ladders propped against the walls. Their footsteps echoed as they crossed the uncarpeted hall and went through a rear door to the kitchen. The room contained only a table and a few plain wooden chairs, a gas stove on which simmered a battered coffeepot, and an open larder whose shelves were stacked high with tinned food. A telephone and a small radio transmitter slightly larger than the one worn by the guard at the gate stood on the table.

Two men rose to greet them as they entered. Yakovitz dumped his prisoner in a chair and while one of the men tied the Arab's hands and feet he told them the basic details of what had happened.

The Saint poured himself a cup of coffee and sat in a chair opposite Hakim. The Arab was wide awake now, and Simon could see the fear behind the defiant set of his features. It was a unique experience, for him, to have the privilege of observing a thoroughly terrified terrorist, and after the wanton assault on his home he wouldn't have missed it for anything.

"So what do we do now?" he enquired genially. "Is it going to be castration with red-hot spoons or a simple force-feeding with boiling oil? Or do you boys have something more scientific to offer?"

He saw Hakim's larnyx take a gulp, and grinned encouragingly.

"Don't worry, Abdul, old camel. They tell me you don't give a damn after the third hour."

Neither of the two Israelis on duty had previously paid much attention to the Saint, assuming that he was merely Yakovitz's aide and therefore a minor member of their organisation. They looked enquiringly at Yakovitz, who grudgingly related the Saint's rôle before and during Hakim's capture. The Saint acknowledged the account with a bow, and the other two agents regarded him with new respect but no extravagant display of friendship.

"As I said, what happens now?" Simon repeated.

Yakovitz smiled faintly, as if he had already been framing the answer to the Saint's question. The way in which the other two men reacted to him showed that he was their superior, and he was obviously enjoying being in charge for the time being, instead of acting as just an assistant to Leila and the Saint.

"That does not concern you, Mr. Templar," he said. "Your job is now completed. You have done us great service, and I am sure our government will show its appreciation. I now arrange for you to be taken back to London."

The Saint shook his head.

"You forget that this is now my game too," he returned calmly. "After last night I've got a personal score to settle with Masrouf and his cronies, and if Hakim the Horrible can tell us anything about where I may be able to find them, then I want to hear it. Also, the way I see it, my job isn't completed until I know that Captain Zabin is safe. She should have telephoned here before we arrived, and obviously she hasn't. So I think I'll just hang around."

Yakovitz's face reddened at the challenge to his authority.

"You are not permitted to do anything except what you are

told. Any action you take against Masrouf is your business, but I am afraid you cannot stay here."

The Saint stretched out his legs and settled more comfortably into his chair.

"And which of you is going to be the first to try and move me?" he queried interestedly.

He appreciated that he was actually in no position to argue with whatever Yakovitz decided. One against three were odds he had tackled before, but even with his supreme confidence in his own abilities he recognised the fact that they were armed and probably trained in unarmed combat as well. His one real hope of staying was that Yakovitz was unsure of the limits of his authority.

Yakovitz hesitated, conscious that his men were looking to him for a lead, but whatever that directive would have been was never known. The radio on the table buzzed and Yakovitz flicked a switch.

"Yes?"

The voice of the guard at the gate made itself heard above the crackle of static.

"Colonel Garvi has arrived, sir."

Yakovitz almost visibly deflated as he realised that his rôle was about to revert once again to that of a subordinate.

Simon smiled.

"Well, perhaps we should wait and let the good colonel decide what's to be done with me."

There was about a minute of awkward silence before Garvi strode into the room. He looked first at Hakim and then at Yakovitz and the Saint.

"You have both done very well," he said.

"We try to please," murmured the Saint ironically.

Yakovitz began to give his report on the morning's events, but the colonel cut him short.

"I know, I know. Masrouf telephoned the embassy. They

have Captain Zabin. They want to do a deal, an exchange of prisoners."

It was no more than the Saint had dreaded to hear, but the confirmation of his fears brought an empty feeling to the pit of his stomach.

"What did you say?" he asked.

"I stalled, there was nothing else I could do. I arranged for them to contact me here, after I had verified that you had Hakim." His gaze travelled from his watch to the telephone. "They should be coming through soon. But Simon, there can only be one answer. An exchange is out of the question. Hakim is too important."

The Saint stood up, and his eyes slashed like a sword through the middle of the other's sentence.

"And Leila? What about her? Or is she expendable for the good of the cause?"

Garvi turned away and stared down at Hakim. When he faced Simon again he was markedly paler and looked years older than he had twenty-four hours before. In any other circumstances the Saint might have felt sorry for him for the decision he had had to make.

"If it were just a matter of a life for a life, I might have to agree. But it is not that simple. The information that this man can give us may save hundreds of lives. Innocent lives. Captain Zabin understood this, she knew the risks when she volunteered for the job. I know her, Simon. I know her far better than you do, and I know she would not thank us for saving her if that was the price we had to pay."

"So you're not even going to give her a chance, Colonel."

Garvi replied softly, almost pleading for understanding: "Simon, I have no choice."

The shrill ringing of the phone split the tense atmosphere in the room. Before anyone else could move, the Saint snatched up the transceiver. He held up his other hand for silence as he waited for the caller to speak first.

"Garvi?"

"Yes."

The Saint knew that his mimicking of the colonel's tone would not have fooled anyone for long, but he was gambling that the call to the embassy had been the first time the terrorists had spoken to their chief enemy.

The caller appeared satisfied. He spoke quickly and with such a thick accent that it was all the Saint could do to make out his words:

"This is the last call you will receive. Either you agree to an exchange, or Captain Zabin dies."

"How do I know she's still alive?"

There was a long pause, and the Saint began to fear that the caller had hung up. Then suddenly Leila's voice came over the line, the words tumbling out as she tried to get her message across before she was silenced.

"Simon, forget me. Keep Hakim. Make him talk."

The sound of a scuffle followed before the Arab spoke again.

"Satisfied? If you want her back, come to Waterloo Bridge tonight at eight. A car will be parked in the middle of the bridge facing north. Stop and flash your lights three times, then follow it. Do exactly as you are told. Understand?"

"Yes."

The phone went dead, and Simon dropped the handset back into its cradle. He looked at Garvi.

"I've agreed to a deal," he stated flatly.

"You cannot complete it. You have no authority."

Yakovitz was standing on the Saint's left but looking towards his boss; his coat was unbuttoned, and Simon could clearly see the automatic in its shoulder holster. The Saint moved so swiftly that no one was aware of his intention until it was too late. As his fingers closed around the butt and pulled the gun from its spring clip, he stepped back and placed himself where he could cover all four men at the same time.

"How's this for authority?" he suggested mildly. "And if any of you have an idea that I don't know how to use it, you can ask the colonel for a reference."

"Simon, don't be a fool." Garvi was rigidly unemotional. "You'll never get out of the grounds. And even if you did manage it somehow, you couldn't take Hakim with you."

"Colonel," said the Saint, just as reasonably, "the name of this game seems to be catch the hostage. If your men know you'll be the first to cash in, they won't be so quick to start shooting. Now, there is one thing I could do. I could blow the lid off this whole illegal operation. I could create a stink that'd smell from Whitehall to the Wailing Wall. But that isn't my idea at all." He paused for a moment, deliberately, and they waited. They had very little option; but now he held their attention with more than the gun in his hand.

"We are going to do exactly what they told me. We are going to take Hakim along and swap him for Leila. They've given me no choice and I'm giving you none. But the rendezvous isn't until eight. That gives us four hours to work out a plan. And four hours for me to find Leila and get her away. It shouldn't be completely beyond us."

Garvi seemed suddenly more relaxed, as if he almost welcomed the Saint's pre-emptive intervention.

"Very well, Simon," he said quietly. "Put the gun away. We'll play it your way—until eight."

"Your word, Colonel?"

"You have it."

Simon lowered the automatic, but tucked it into his belt instead of returning it to Yakovitz. Garvi accepted the Saint's reservation without comment.

"We also have four hours to find out what we can from our prisoner," he remarked.

"Help yourselves," said the Saint hospitably. "Just don't do anything that leaves marks, in case he has to be exhibited."

Hakim had been following the action and dialogue in swivel-eyed silence, but now he protested for the first time.

"You cannot make me talk. They would kill me."

Yakovitz cuffed him across the ear with the back of his hand.

"If they don't, I might," he snarled. "Keep your mouth shut until I tell you to open it."

He was about to say more when the phone rang again, and Garvi picked it up. He listened for a moment and then held it out to the Saint.

"For you. Someone who seems to expect you to be here."

Simon took over the instrument.

"Harry?" The bite in his voice was belied by the sparkle in his eyes. "What the hell happened to you? Where are you?"

Harry's reply came in an injured whine.

"That was unfair, Mr. Templar. You didn't say nothin' about a shooting match. I was goin' to clear off when I see them grab the girl, so I followed. I couldn't call you before in case I lost them."

"Where are you?"

"It's goin' to cost, Mr. Templar. This ain't what you ordered originally."

"Tell me where the girl is, and I'll give you enough to keep the bookies singing until Christmas."

"Straight?"

"Straight. Now make it snappy."

"They've taken her to an old factory, back of the Union Canal in Bethnal Green."

"How many are they?"

"Five, I think. There was the three that brought her an' another two met 'em when they arrived. Might be more inside for all I know."

"Right. Stay with them, Harry. I'll be there as soon as I can —in a couple of hours with luck. Tell me exactly where this place is."

When he was sure that he could find the hideout, Simon hung up and turned to the others.

"Gentlemen," he announced happily, "we are in business."

10

The Saint pressed his foot down and the big car surged forward on the instant that an obstructive traffic light turned green. For the first time since he had been summoned to the embassy and become involved in a duel that was not of his choosing, he felt relaxed and in total control of his actions. The events of the day had combined to uncomplicate the proceedings. The hunt was over, the intrigue finished. The whole affair had been stripped of its complexities and clutter and reduced to the basics upon which an adventurer builds the structure of his career. There were villains to be thwarted and a damsel in distress to be rescued. He asked for nothing better.

The plan he had settled on with Garvi after Harry's call was the essence of simplicity, and if he was aware that its execution would prove more difficult than its conception he did not allow the thought to worry him. Garvi and Yakovitz would take Hakim to the bridge and follow the terrorists to their hideout where the exchange would be made. As the rendezvous was taking place, he would enter the factory alone and try to get Leila out while the garrison was at least reduced.

Garvi's only rider had been that if anything went wrong he would keep Hakim and leave both the Saint and Leila to their fates, and Simon had agreed to it. Secure in the knowledge that Garvi would not double-cross him now, he had taken the time for a quick snack before leaving. Unlike Napoleon's quoted army, he did not necessarily march on his stomach, but he knew that no man's efficiency is improved by the hypoglycemia of hunger.

Although bent on making the best time he could, he scrupulously observed every speed limit and traffic regulation. To be stopped for any technical infringement would more than cancel out the few minutes he might have gained. He had left Garvi the Hirondel, as it would be more easily recognised by the terrorists, and had taken instead the embassy Mercedes, from which he had removed the conspicuous "CD" badge. Now with the cool breeze fanning his cheek through the open window he even hummed a tune, and the eyes that swept the road ahead were bright with the light of battle.

His hands caressed the wheel as he drove along the long straight stretches of Forest Road. The headlights bored a tunnel through the twilight, throwing the trees along the roadside into sharp silhouette; beyond them there might have been nothing at all. The blood seemed to throb through his veins as if keeping in time with the roar of the engine. All too soon open road was left behind, and he was forced to cut his speed as he entered the East London suburbs and followed Harry's directions towards his goal.

It was nearing seven-thirty by the time he reached his destination and glided to a standstill behind Harry's van. He made a rapid final check of the automatic he had taken from Yakovitz before climbing out of the car and taking stock of his surroundings.

The district, in the grandiose language of the local authority, was scheduled for redevelopment, and consequently they had blitzed it more effectively than the Luftwaffe could ever have done, and then, for some reason known only to the planners who decide such things, had left it alone and apparently forgotten about it.

Acres of rubble now stretched where once there had been houses, shops, and a community of people. Fences made of old doors sectioned off what had once been blocks of buildings. The streets that ran between them were no more than continuous lines of potholes; the pavements were cracked and broken, and in some parts had ceased to exist altogether. What few buildings remained standing were often without roofs or windows, and no one had bothered to repair the street lamps that had long since been shattered by itinerant vandals.

Simon walked slowly around the next corner, keeping to the shadow of the fence as he waited for Harry to show himself.

"Psst!"

He stopped and looked around but there was no way of telling where the sifflation had come from.

"Over here," croaked a hoarse voice.

This time he managed to locate its source, and stepped through a gap in the fence to where Harry-the-Nose was standing. Harry beckoned the Saint to follow him across to the far side of the site, where he clambered up to the top of a pile of rubble and the Saint joined him.

From there it was possible to see over the top of the next hoarding, and they had a clear field of vision on every side.

"You took your time, Mr. Templar," Harry said aggrievedly. "I'm starving, I ain't had nothing for hours."

"My stomach bleeds for you," commiserated the Saint. "Where are they?"

Harry pointed to a large building that the bulldozers appeared to have missed.

"Over there. I saw a light on the third floor about half an hour ago, but nothing since."

"Any comings or goings?"

"Two of 'em left in a car about five minutes before you got 'ere. But the twist wasn't with 'em."

Simon Templar drew a deep satisfied breath.

"Okay, Harry, you've done a good job. I'll recommend you for a Star of David."

"That's fine, Mr. Templar," Harry said. "But what about me money?"

"Tomorrow night, usual place, same time. Now toddle off and get some food."

The man needed no further prompting. The Saint waited until he had heard the van's engine splutter into life before he swung himself over the fence and started towards the building Harry had indicated.

What had seemed at first like a profligate squandering of priceless time now justified itself; the dusk had finally deepened into dark, and the operation that he contemplated cried out for the co-operation of nightfall. Furthermore, now that two of the Ungodly had set off in plenty of time to meet the deadline on Waterloo Bridge, the numerical odds against him had been significantly reduced.

And it still wasn't going to be easy.

The factory was a perfect example of Victorian utility architecture at its most hideous, but he needed only a brief look to understand its attractions for the terrorists. It stood four storeys tall, surrounded by high walls on three sides and flush with the canal on the fourth. Between the factory and its perimeter boundaries was a wide courtyard, the whole of which was clearly visible from any of the windows at the front. The building itself was flat-fronted and featureless except for the rows of small barred windows that marked the different levels of the floors, giving it more the look of a prison than a place of work. Not, he reflected wryly, that there was probably much difference between the two when the towering chimneys at either end of the building had belched smoke for the first time.

The only entrance to the courtyard was through a wide archway, and there was nothing between it and the factory that even a cat could have used for cover. The Saint considered the problem.

"Looks like we have to risk getting wet," he decided.

He picked his way carefully between the piles of rubble and knee-high nettles, and followed the wall around the side of the factory until he reached the canal.

The water was blacker than the sky and smelt like an unventilated sewer. The bank was littered with chunks of rusting iron, rotting furniture, and heaps of assorted household refuse. The top of an old car was just visible above the top of the water.

The rear of the factory rose sheer from the water's edge, except for the crumbling remains of a short wooden jetty in the centre and a narrow catwalk that linked it with each end of the building. Above it on every floor were doorways, each with its own hoist, that had once served to transfer the company's goods to and from the canal barges.

The rear wall of the building looked ready to slide into the water the first time a stiff wind blew, but the chance of a fall was less uninviting than the probability of collecting a bullet in a frontal assault, and he saw little attraction in being the moving target in a shooting gallery. He stepped onto the catwalk, pressed his back against the wall, and started to edge sideways towards the jetty.

The stone under his feet had been worn smooth by the weather, and the subsidence of the building had caused the ledge to tilt downwards so that every step was an individual performance in the art of balancing that would not have disgraced a tightrope walker. The Saint pressed the flat of his hands against the wall, drawing an absurd sense of security from the feel of his fingers probing the shallow cracks between the bricks, in the same way that a soldier under shellfire hides behind a bush.

His progress was agonizingly slow, and all the while he was aware that time was ticking away. With every minute spent trying to find a way in, his chances of reaching Leila and getting out again before the terrorists arrived back diminished. At one spot a yard of the ledge had completely broken away, and he had to turn on his toes until he was facing the wall and search for crevices in the brickwork large enough for him to curl his fingers into. He stepped into space supported only by the fingertips of one hand while his other desperately tried to find a similar hold. A loose brick dislodged by his probing slid from the wall and landed with a splash in the water below, and then his foot touched the ledge again and he was able to take the strain from the muscles of his hand and arm.

The ledge widened as it reached the jetty and he was able to turn sideways onto the wall as he tested the strength of the planking by pushing out one leg and slowly lowering his weight onto it. The board creaked in protest but held. He glanced at his watch and was shocked to learn that it had taken him nearly fifteen minutes to travel twice that number of yards. It was a quarter to eight. Already the rendezvous would have taken place and in fifteen minutes, possibly less, they would have arrived back.

Two heavy doors led from the jetty into the factory. A thick iron chain and padlock had been passed through the handles and he swore swiftly as he knelt and examined the barrier. Despite the thick coating of rust it was still strong enough to resist anything short of a sledgehammer. The handles themselves offered brighter prospects. They too were of iron, but much older and more corroded than the chain, and the wood to which they were fixed was badly rotted. They moved slightly when he pulled against them with both hands, and he glanced around desperately for anything that could be used as a lever.

At each end of the jetty were fixed wooden posts about four feet high that had once supported a gate designed to prevent sacks slipping into the canal. He grasped the top of the nearest one, spreading his legs apart and bending his knees to brace himself, and applied every ounce of his strength as he pulled. The post tore free of its fastening, and he toppled backwards and only just managed to stop himself tumbling off the platform.

He slipped the post through the door handle, placed one foot against the door, and threw his whole weight backwards.

The handle took a jagged square of wood with it as it came away with a crash that splintered the still night air like a gunshot, at the same time dragging the door open.

The Saint slipped through the gap and into the factory, drawing his gun as he went.

He found himself in a high-ceilinged room that appeared to take up the whole of the ground floor. The only light was provided by the pale rays of the moon that filtered through the glassless windows high above his head. Beside the jetty doors a stone staircase curved upwards to link with the floors above, and he waited at the foot of it until his eyes became accustomed to the gloom.

It was impossible for the noise of his entrance not to have been heard by the men in the building. But there was a fair chance that they would attribute it to the spontaneous collapse of one of the rotting timbers, or to some outside happening, instead of to a break-in. Harry had indicated the third floor at the front, and if they were still there they might not have been able to identify the sound accurately. At any rate, that was what he had to hope for.

He climbed the stairs to the next floor without incident. It was similar to the one below, except that the ceiling was lower and he could just make out partitioned sections at one end that had previously served as offices.

On the second floor, the staircase led to a corridor, and he followed it to the front of the building. The boards creaked as he moved although he kept close to the wall, unable in the half light to determine whether the darker patches in the centre of the passage were merely pools of shadow or holes. He glanced into the rooms on either side, but all were empty and derelict and in many the floor had partially collapsed and he could see through to the floor below. The corridor merged into another wider one that ran the length of the front of the building to a staircase at either end. His watch showed 8:05 as he turned left and quickened his step.

If punctuality was any virtue of guerillas, the Waterloo Bridge contact should already have been made.

He took the stairs two at a time and was on the halfway

landing when the noise of a door slamming somewhere immediately above made him freeze in mid-stride. The beam of a torch stabbed a circle of light on the wall above his head and grew wider as the man approached. Bending almost double, Simon leapt up the remaining steps. The man was no more than a dozen feet from the top of the stairs. Crouched by the wall, the Saint held his breath as he waited for him to draw level.

A rat scuffled somewhere in the darkness below, and the man stopped and turned his head. The Saint needed no better invitation.

He stepped out directly into the man's path.

"Good evening," he said courteously.

The man's mouth opened, but whether to emit an equally well-mannered reply or shout the Saint did not wait to find out. His fist swung upwards with a force that lifted the recipient off his feet, and the Saint caught him as he fell and lowered him gently to the ground, prising the torch from his grasp in the process.

"And then there were two," he observed to his strictly personal audience.

A ribbon of light beneath a door at the far end of the passage indicated his destination. Now he did not bother to muffle the sound of his approach, confident that the men inside would assume that it was their colleague returning. He turned the handle and entered as casually as if he were in his own home.

Leila sat in a chair in the centre of the room, her arms and legs tightly bound. Khaldun was at the window looking down into the courtyard, while another man whom the Saint had not seen before sat on an upturned packing case cleaning a rifle.

Khaldun turned as the door opened, and at the sight of the Saint recoiled as if he had been hit. The rifleman dropped his cloth and stared in amazement. Only Leila managed to contain her surprise.

"I thought you were never going to get here," she said calmly.

The Saint smiled.

"You didn't leave a forwarding address," he complained. "Excuse me . . ."

His automatic barked, and the rifle flew from its cleaner's grip and clattered to the floor with the Saint's bullet embedded in its stock.

"That was your first and only warning," he said quietly. "Both of you face down on the floor, now. Move!"

The men did as they were told, and he knelt between them to relieve Khaldun of a revolver and his companion of a small, snub-nosed automatic. He put both guns in his pockets as he stood up. Without taking his eyes off the two men, he untied Leila's wrists and gave her the automatic to control the situation while he freed her legs.

"Have either of these specimens done anything to you?" he asked gently.

Leila shook her head as she vigorously rubbed the circulation back into her arms and flexed her legs.

"No. I think they were keeping that for later."

"What was the plan?"

"When Hakim arrived, I was to walk across the courtyard towards him so that it would look as if they were keeping their bargain. As soon as we met in the middle they were going to start shooting--Khaldun and this one up here with rifles, another of them downstairs, plus the two in the car."

"Quite an ambush," Simon observed reflectively. "It seems almost a pity to spoil it."

While she kept the two Arabs covered, he picked up the lengths of rope that had bound her, and expertly tied the new captives together, passing the cords from their ankles and wrists behind their backs to finish around their necks. He regarded his handiwork with grim satisfaction.

"You can have great fun trying to unravel yourselves," he told them, "though I wouldn't try too hard if I were you. One pull in the wrong direction, and you'll find that breathing is only a memory."

The two men lay perfectly still, and the Saint's smile widened as he bowed and touched his forehead and lips in the traditional salute.

"Maha-ssaláama," he murmured with genial derision, and turned back to Leila. "Come on, darling—let's keep that date."

He led the way down the stairs to the front door and pulled it open, and they stood together just inside the opening.

"Simon," she said huskily, "I don't know how you got here, but it was so wonderful—"

The roar of two approaching cars cut off her words. The station wagon swung into the courtyard, but the Hirondel stopped just outside the entrance. Yakovitz and Hakim climbed out and stood beside it; Garvi himself got out of the driving seat. The Red Sabbath car pulled up a few yards from the factory door.

The Saint pressed his lips to Leila's ear.

"Do just as they told you," he whispered. "And good luck."

Leila took his hand off her shoulder, giving it a tight squeeze, and began to walk towards the centre of the courtyard as Hakim approached awkwardly from the other side. The converging headlights of the Hirondel and the wagon lit up the scene like a macabre stage set.

There was only a yard between Leila and Hakim when the Saint yelled: "Now!"

Leila brought up her automatic and pushed it into Hakim's chest. The terrorist wavered in blank bewilderment, but whatever she said combined with the menace of the gun to make him turn and run back towards the courtyard entrance with her at his heels.

In the same instant that he shouted the Saint had also moved. He burst out of the doorway with a gun in each hand, firing at the station wagon. Having heard the terrorists' plan, he was more concerned with creating a diversion that would get Leila Zabin to safety than with making target scores. He saw the wagon's windscreen shatter, but it was impossible to tell if either of the men inside was hit. But even if unscathed, they could only have been in a state of shock after finding themselves the targets instead of part of the supporting fire.

Simon only paused in his run across the courtyard to place a bullet accurately in each of the station wagon's front tires.

He saw Yakovitz bundling Hakim into the back of the Hirondel, as Garvi opened the front passenger door for Leila. The Saint grabbed Garvi by the arm.

"You in the back, too!" he snapped. "I'll drive."

He threw himself in behind the wheel and hit the accelerator in one continuous movement, to take the car hurtling away.

11

The Hirondel—if any fault in such a classic vehicle can be acknowledged—was never designed to be a family car, adaptable to the transport of friends, relatives, and/or assorted offspring. The nominal rear seat might, at a pinch, have accommodated a couple of not too well-nourished children; but with the combination of Yakovitz, Hakim, and Garvi the pinch became a highly painful compression. But their ordeal lasted less than a minute, while the Saint whisked them around to where he had left Garvi's Mercedes. There was no pursuit from the factory.

"You'd better take your own car back," he said as he braked behind it, "even if it won't be so cosy."

While Yakovitz, as poker-faced as ever, hustled Hakim into the back of the Mercedes, Garvi found a moment to smile.

"Well done, Simon. You too, Captain. You both gave me some very worrying moments back there. What happened?"

The Saint condensed the account of his actions up to the moment when Leila had started her walk across the courtyard into three rapid sentences.

"I'll keep Leila for company," he concluded. "But I'll stay on your tail back to Epping—just in case of anything."

Following the rear lights of Garvi's car, Simon drove mechanically without consciously noticing the route as his mind raced ahead to consider questions that still had to be answered. Leila sat silently beside him with her eyes closed, and he wondered just how much the events of the day had cost her in terms of stamina.

Although there could have been no contest either between drivers or their automobiles, Garvi set a fast pace, and they were soon swinging off the highway and bumping along the narrow track towards the house. The Saint glanced at his watch as he brought the Hirondel to a halt outside the gates and waited a moment for the guards to identify Garvi and let them in. He was surprised to see that there were still several minutes left before nine o'clock.

Leila opened her eyes and sat upright as he parked the car in the driveway. He speculated whether she had slept or if she too had been considering the prospects ahead. She gave him no clue as she turned her head to look at him, but her voice was strangely distant and once again he had a sense of barriers being raised between them.

"I have not thanked you for coming to my rescue," she said.

He leant across and kissed her, but there was little response from her lips.

"Let's call that a down deposit," he suggested lightly, but she did not return his smile.

"Simon, when this is over . . ." she began hesitantly, but he cut her short by placing a finger against her lips. The gesture recalled the previous night, and the memory brought back the same disquieting emotions he had felt then.

"We'll worry about it later," he said softly, and pointed towards Garvi and Yakovitz, who were half dragging, half carrying Hakim up the steps. "Come on, or they'll start the party without us."

They filed into the house and gathered in one of the downstairs rooms. The dust sheets had been removed and the ladders and paint pots tidied away in a hurried attempt to make it habitable. A trolley laden with sandwiches and drinks had been added to the furnishings.

Yakovitz kept as close to Hakim as his own shadow, but the terrorist was clearly in no condition to cause any further trouble. His steps faltered, and his head lolled against his shoulder as if it was too heavy for him to support. He looked around through clouded, uncomprehending eyes, and offered no protest when Yakovitz pushed him roughly into a chair, but simply slumped forward with his head cradled on his knees. Yakovitz stood behind him while Leila sat in an armchair opposite. One of the agents the Saint had seen in the kitchen during the afternoon followed them into the room and took up a position with his back to the door.

The Saint poured himself a drink and handed Garvi a similarly stiff measure of malt. He regarded Hakim with detached interest as he asked: "How long before he starts singing again?"

"Not long," Garvi replied grimly. "One more injection should be sufficient. I will attend to it personally."

Simon selected a sandwich and took an experimental bite.

"Well, if you'll excuse me, I'll leave you to it," he yawned. "It's been a busy day, and I could use a little peace and quiet. Let me know as soon as you've finished."

Garvi nodded, and the man at the door stood aside.

The Saint went out and found an adjacent room whose furnishings included a sofa of sufficient size for his length. After finishing his sandwich and his drink, he stretched himself out and in a few seconds had dropped into a light but restful sleep.

He slept because it seemed the most intelligent way to spend the time. The only alternative would have been to attend the interrogation; and although he cared nothing about the procedure to which Hakim was being subjected, neither would he have derived any pleasure from the spectacle. But in anticipation of what further activities might be to come, even his tungsten constitution would be refreshed by a nap.

Peacefully as he slept, his eyes flicked open the second the door handle turned, and he was standing by the time Garvi reached the centre of the room. His watch informed him that he had been asleep for only a little over an hour, but he was as alert and clear-headed as any cat roused from its nap by the smell of a mouse.

Answering the Saint's unspoken question, Garvi said: "We have what we wanted. It was quicker than I expected, but despair frequently helps to lower the subject's resistance. Right now we are checking the names he gave us. They have been relayed to the embassy, and from there they can be confirmed with Tel Aviv."

"How long will it be before you're certain that Hakim has spilled the real barbecue beans?"

"Another half hour at the most."

"So soon?" the Saint queried in surprise.

"Much of what he said only confirmed what we already suspected but he has supplied many details we needed. And the filing system at my headquarters is very efficient."

"I'm sure it is, Colonel," Simon concurred. "But what happens once you're satisfied that Hakim has no more haricots to unload?"

Garvi shrugged.

"He is of no further use to us," he answered carelessly.

"But he's still a problem," the Saint insisted; and before Garvi could reply, he continued: "You can't take him back to Israel for a show trial, however much you might like to, because if you did there'd by no way you could hide the extent of your activities in London—an illegal operation, remember. And while the British Government would probably be pleased at the outcome, they couldn't do anything but condemn the methods used, and your bosses won't want to risk a diplomatic incident.

So the only practical alternative is a concrete swimsuit and a midnight dip in the Thames. Am I right?"

"Whatever we decide, Simon," Garvi hedged, "I promise you won't be implicated."

The Saint snorted derisively with a scornful laugh.

"The hell with *being* implicated, I *am* implicated! I was implicated the moment Yakovitz and his buddy hijacked me at the airport. You've got what you wanted. As far as you're concerned, the operation has been one hundred per cent successful and it's all because of me. Now you can settle the account. I want the last act left in my hands."

Their stares crossed like rapiers—the Saint's intense and unyielding; Garvi's suspicious, uncertain.

"What do you have in mind?" Garvi asked.

"You've got what you wanted from Hakim, but that doesn't mean you've forgiven his former comrades. And neither have I. I have this odd prejudice against people who try to blow me up and destroy my property," the Saint explained.

"But your plan?"

Simon smiled.

"You know what they say, Colonel. If you want to shoot a tiger, tether a goat."

When he had finished outlining his scheme, Garvi shook his head doubtfully.

"It's a risk, Simon."

"So is crossing the road," the Saint retorted, and before Garvi could begin to put forward objections he turned on his heel and walked towards the door. "Let's have a look at the goat."

They went back to the room where the interrogation had been completed. Hakim sat in a chair with his chin on his chest, completely oblivious to his surroundings. Leila and Yakovitz were sitting at a table sipping black coffee. The Saint pulled Hakim's head up so that he could look into his face.

"Do you have something in that medicine kit of yours that

will bring him back to the land of the living quickly?" he asked Garvi.

The Israeli looked puzzled.

"Yes. But it would mean a large dose, and that could be dangerous, even fatal."

"Your sudden concern for the patient is very touching," Simon commented sarcastically. "Give it to him. I want him back in working order as soon as possible."

Yakovitz looked questioningly at his superior, but Garvi only nodded.

"Do as he says," he instructed; and with ill-concealed reluctance the agent opened a doctor's-type black satchel and began to fill a syringe.

The Saint rummaged through the small pile of Hakim's effects that were spread out on the table, and finally found what he sought written on the back of a snapshot of Yasmina.

As he did so the phone rang, and Garvi answered it. The colonel listened intently for a few minutes, and smiled thinly at the Saint and Leila as he replaced the receiver.

"We have a report from Tel Aviv," he informed them. "Everything he has told us checks out."

"Good," said the Saint, and took over the telephone. He began to dial the number on the back of the snapshot. "Then you agree to let me take over, Colonel?"

Garvi compressed his lips.

"I agree. At your own risk."

"It seems to me I've been at my own risk most of the time," said the Saint amicably.

Then the number was ringing, and in a minute or so a feminine voice answered.

"Yasmina?" he said, and on receiving the hesitant confirmation, he went on in a studiously impersonal tone: "I am calling for your friend Abdul Hakim. He is being released by the people who detained him. He wishes you to join him in going to a safe place. Do you know the Highgate Cemetery—did he ever show you the tomb of Karl Marx there?"

"Yes." The response was scarcely audible, and he felt a twinge of pity for her as he pictured her in the shabby flat where she lived.

"Good. Go there. At four o'clock this morning. Exactly. Hakim will be waiting for you. After that, everything will be as Allah wills. Understand?"

"Yes . . . but . . ."

The Saint hung up and looked across at Hakim. Whatever stimulant Yakovitz had pumped into him appeared to be having a miraculous effect. He was sitting upright now and looking at his surroundings in the hazy way of someone roughly aroused from a deep sleep, but it was unlikely that he had heard or understood much of the conversation.

"Officially, I have heard nothing, and I know nothing," Garvi said expressionlessly. "Captain Zabin and Yakovitz may volunteer to stay with you, on the same understanding. Unfortunately I cannot do the same. It would be most embarrassing politically if anything went wrong and I was seen to be involved. But whenever you want, you can contact me at the embassy."

Simon Templar regarded him with a touch of quizzical challenge.

"Is that all you can say, Leon?" he taunted.

Colonel Garvi hesitated for one second, and then held out his hand.

"Mazel tov," he said.

12

London's Highgate Cemetery is a horror-film producer's dream. Victorian Gothic memorials to mortality cracked open by the weather vainly strive to rise above a wilderness of tall grass and tangled shrubs. Even in daytime it is a lonely and desolate spot, but in the pre-dawn moonlight it becomes charged with a sinister atmosphere of its own that can be felt by even the most cynical and unsuperstitious realist.

Leila shivered involuntarily as she surveyed the scene, but the Saint only grinned as he brought his lips close to her ear and breathed: "Not afraid of ghosties and ghoulies and long-legged beasties, are we?"

She walked disdainfully away from the teasing voice and was the first to go through the gates. Simon reached her side in a couple of long strides and led the way along the maze of overgrown paths between tombs and headstones. Yakovitz brought up the rear, prodding Hakim forward with the business end of his automatic.

The Arab was completely recovered by now, and the scent of possible freedom had made him excited and nervous, although they had told him nothing except that he was to meet Yasmina as a reward for his co-operation.

The tomb of Karl Marx consists of a pillar on which is mounted a massive stone head which, with its flowing beard and wild hair makes him look more like an Old Testament patriarch than an instigator of revolution. He lies snugly at rest, surrounded in death by the Victorian capitalists and imperialists whom he loathed so much in life. The area immediately around the pillar is always carefully maintained, and attracts more pilgrims than the average saint's shrine. With floral tributes strewn at its feet, the monument to the man who regarded religion as the opium of the people takes on an incongruous air of holiness.

Simon Templar stopped and gave it an irreverent salute. "Good morning, Karl," he murmured. "I've brought along one of your disciples to pay his respects."

Yakovitz pushed Hakim forward so violently that he lost his footing and sprawled at the base of the pillar. The Saint looked down at him with a cynical smile playing at the corners of his mouth.

"No need to overdo the kowtowing," he drawled. "Just a polite bow would have done."

Hakim picked himself up and brushed the dirt from his clothes as he glanced anxiously around.

"Where is Yasmina?" he demanded accusingly. "You said she would be here."

"Don't worry, she will be," Simon replied, and glanced at the luminous dial of his watch. "In less than ten minutes, if she's punctual. I'm sure it will be a very moving reunion, so we'll withdraw to a discreet distance."

He was turning away when Hakim called him back, his apprehension clearly sounding in his voice.

"You are going to leave me here alone?"

Simon gazed at him with cold contempt.

"I thought you'd feel comfortably at home surrounded by death. It's your favourite scene, isn't it? Anyhow, Yasmina will soon be here to hold your hand. But if you try to move away before she arrives, I shall take great pleasure in kicking you back."

Without giving the other time to reply, the Saint turned again and walked away down the path with Leila and Yakovitz a step behind him.

As soon as they had rounded a corner and were out of Hakim's line of sight, he stopped and indicated positions to them from which they would be able to keep watch on Hakim and the area around the Karl Marx memorial.

Simon himself moved off at a tangent, and circled back as silently as a cautious cat among the shadows, flitting like a wraith from tomb to tomb until he was so close to Hakim that he could even hear the terrorist breathing. The night seemed to swallow him as wholly and completely as a ghost.

He stood as still as the headstone beside him as the minutes dragged by, while Hakim paced up and down, only two or three jerky steps each way, starting in alarm every time the wind rustled the grass.

At last the Saint's sensitive ears picked up the kind of sound he had been waiting for. It was no more than the faint crunch of a dry twig, but it told him that the first part of his plan had succeeded. By sound alone he followed Yasmina's progress down the path; but Hakim, confused and frightened, did not see her until she rounded the nearest corner.

At the sight of her lover she began to run.

"Abdul! Abdul!"

Yasmina stumbled into the Arab's outstretched arms, crying with relief, holding him tightly as if she feared he would vanish if she released him.

Simon hardly spared the couple a glance. He was looking past the girl, towards the bend in the path around which she had come, and silently drew his automatic and eased off the safety catch as he heard other footsteps approaching.

This time Hakim also heard them. He stared in wide-eyed panic as Masrouf, Khaldun, and one of the men who had helped to guard Leila at the factory appeared.

Masrouf walked in the centre flanked by his two aides and the guns of all three were drawn and aimed directly at Hakim. Yasmina turned and screamed.

"No! No!"

"Stand aside, Yasmina," Masrouf commanded. "We do not want to hurt you."

Hakim released the girl, but she did not move.

In the same chilling voice of a judge pronouncing sentence Masrouf continued: "Abdul Hakim, you are a traitor to the cause and to your people."

Masrouf raised his gun, and the action snapped Hakim from the spell that had transfixed him from the moment he had caught sight of the three men. In the same instant that Masrouf's finger tightened on the trigger, he grabbed Yasmina and pulled her backwards to cover his body with hers.

The bullet entered just above her heart. She opened her mouth as if to scream, but only a whimpered cough escaped before she sagged limply forward.

It was one of the most callous acts of total selfishness that the Saint had ever been forced to witness. And since he could only hold himself responsible, in essence, for having made it happen, the first duty of vengeance had been abruptly bequeathed to him.

He felt his blood turn to slow rivers of ice, and he fired.

A neat black-rimmed hole appeared in Hakim's forehead. Yasmina slipped from his grasp and he pitched over, falling across her body, and lay still.

Masrouf spun around and fired wildly in the direction of the Saint, but the bullets zipped harmlessly above Simon's head. The Saint took careful aim again, but before he could fire, Leila and Yakovitz opened up from the positions where he had left them. Khaldun clutched at his belly, floundered, and went down. The third terrorist had barely started to run when a bullet bowled him over like a rag doll. Masrouf, somehow unscathed by the fusillade, was still searching blindly for a target when the Saint released his last shot with no more compunction than the grenade that had been flung through the window of his living room the night before.

13

The electric light was weak against the strengthening sun and the room was chilly. In Kensington Gardens, outside the embassy, first one bird and then another heralded the morning until the air was ringing with their song. The Saint stared silently at the black liquid in his cup while Leila finished her report.

Garvi turned to the Saint and smiled.

"So your plan worked out perfectly," he said. "It was an ideal ending."

"Tell that to Yasmina," Simon returned stonily, and the smile faded from Garvi's face.

"It was a pity about her, Simon. But she knew the sort of people she was associating with. You knew the risks when you set your trap, but you must not blame yourself for what happened to her."

"Yasmina was Masrouf and Co.'s only remaining link with Hakim," said the Saint. "Having lost him it was a pretty safe bet that they'd go after her again as soon as they'd got their car working again, and follow her when she left her flat. Leila and I used the guns I'd taken from them at the factory, and we swapped guns around before we left so that the police will think it was just a private shoot-out between terrorists."

He rose slowly to his feet, finally allowing the strain of the past two days to show.

"Now if you'll excuse me, Colonel, I must be going home. I've still got to get some redecorations organised. After which I'll be looking forward to keeping my promise to show Leila some of the more cheerful sights of the town, as soon as she feels up to it."

Leila looked away from him, studying her hands and avoiding his eyes. Garvi shifted awkwardly in his chair.

"I'm sorry, Simon," he said, and sounded as if he meant it. "But Captain Zabin is under orders to return at once to Tel Aviv. There is nothing I can do about it."

The Saint walked over to her and gently ruffled her hair. He bent over and kissed her lightly on the lips before walking to the door. He turned and smiled ruefully.

"Some other time, then," he said gently. *"Shalom,* Captain Zabin."

Leila looked up at him and did not try to hide the moisture clouding her eyes.

"L'chayim, Mr. Templar," she whispered.

WATCH FOR THE SIGN

OF THE SAINT

HE WILL BE BACK